What Readers are Saying About *Just in Time*

"History can sometimes be long and tedious. The *Just in Time* books by Cheri Pray Earl and Carol Lynch Williams are short, believable tales that move along quickly with generous doses of suspense and action. Perfect for Common Core curriculums, students will find themselves quickly enveloped in page-turning narratives. A history treat for sure!"

—CARLA MORRIS, Provo City Library Children's Services Manager, member of American Library Association 2004 Caldecott Committee, author of *The Boy Who Was Raised by Librarians* (Peachtree Publications, 2007)

"A little something for everyone—history, humor, adventure, time travel . . ." —*Kirkus Reviews*

"I couldn't stop reading because I wanted to see if George and Gracie would get their mom and dad back."

—VAN, Age 6, Utah

• • •

"This story is like lemonade. Once you start, you can't stop. The story really draws you in, and you don't want to put it down until you're done. A definite 5-star rating!!!"

—BROCK, Age 12, Ohio

• • •

"*Just In Time* is a great series of fun, exciting stories and funny characters. I like when Gracie, George, and the others change into animals."

— BELLE, Age 8, Colorado

JUST IN TIME

For Mathilde, our third girl.

—C.P.E.

And this time for Mom.

—C.L.W.

Published by Familius LLC, www.familius.com

Familius books are available at special discounts for bulk purchases for sales promotions, family or corporate use. Special editions, including personalized covers, excerpts of existing books, or books with corporate logos, can be created in large quantities for special needs. For more information, contact Premium Sales at 559-876-2170 or email specialmarkets@familius.com.

Library of Congress Catalog-in-Publication Data

2014947916
pISBN 978-1-939629-24-1
eISBN 978-1-939629-96-8

Printed in the United States of America

Edited by Amy Stewart
Cover and book design by David Miles

10 9 8 7 6 5 4 3 2 1

First Edition

JUST IN TIME

BOOK 4

A DANGEROUS DAY IN

GEORGIA

CHERI PRAY EARL AND

CAROL LYNCH WILLIAMS

ILLUSTRATIONS BY MANELLE OLIPHANT

FAMILIUS

MEET THE
STOCKTON FAMILY

Matthew
Stockton

Grandpa
Stockton

Laura
Stockton

Gracie   George

AND KEEP YOUR
EYES PEELED
FOR...

Crowe

Charles
Candler

TRACK THE ADVENTURE

 Delaware

 Pennsylvania

 New Jersey

 Georgia

It Happened Like This . . . I Swear

I'm George. And my sister's name is Gracie.

Gracie is nine years old. So am I.

We're twins. I'm older than she is by 5.75 minutes.

She's taller than me by one and a half inches.

But I'm smarter by about two feet.

Me and Gracie live with our grandpa. He's a fix-it man. He works at the Stockton Museum of Just About Everything in American History. Our family's museum.

Mom and Dad used to work here too.

Except we haven't really seen them for two years. Since they found the time machine.

That's when our trouble started.

Mom and Dad used the time machine to travel back in history. They bought great stuff for our museum. Then they got trapped. We never know where they are. Or where they will be. Or when.

We sure miss them. A lot.

Me and Gracie have a plan to get our parents back. We have to return all the stuff they bought for the Stockton Museum. Then Mom and Dad can come home.

The problem is, now *we* have to ride in the time machine.

And we have another big problem. Mr. Crowe.

He's following us.

He wants us to take him to 1879. In our time machine.

If we take him home before we return everything, before we rescue our parents . . . we might never see Mom or Dad again.

Then we might get trapped in time too.

CHAPTER 1

Up, Down, All Around

Me and Gracie stood at the map of the United States. The one on the wall in Grandpa's fix-it shop. In our family's museum.

Gracie traced the state of Georgia with her finger. She looked at me.

"Hey, George. Your shoe's untied," Gracie said. "It's dragging around behind you." She grinned. "Like your rattail in Pennsylvania."

I straightened my glasses. "Yeah, right," I said because Gracie is always saying stuff like that. To make me look. "Don't. Care."

I'd check my shoelace later. When she wasn't watching.

"Okay, fine," Gracie said. "Don't blame me if you trip and break your whiskers ... er ... glasses, I mean."

Grandpa did a "Heeheeheehee" laugh. He stood with his arms folded.

The antique clock ticked in the corner. The minute hand passed midnight.

"What does the map say, Gracie?" Grandpa said. "Where are you and George off to this time?"

She tapped next to the blinking red light. "It says 'St. Simons Island, Georgia, 1942.'" She turned to Grandpa. "I didn't know there was an island in Georgia."

"Four islands, actually," said Grandpa. He frowned. "Hmmm . . . Why can't I remember what your parents bought on that trip?" He walked to his desk and thumbed through his stack of papers. "That would be at the start of World War II," he said.

"World War II?" I said. "Cool."

I tapped the blinking light. Peeked behind the map tacked on the wall. Nothing. I didn't know how that light could work. With no plug. Or batteries. Or even a light bulb.

Gracie stared at Grandpa.

So I sneaked a peek at my shoelace.

"Ha, George. Made you look," said Gracie.

I lifted my head with a jerk. "Nuh-uh."

"What's wrong?" Gracie said. She twisted her locket. The one Mom gave her. She never takes it off.

"Nothing," I said.

"Not you, George," Gracie said.

I turned around.

Grandpa held a paper. He had on his worried face. I walked over to him. Leaned over his arm. And read out loud.

"April 8, 1942: A 1941, red Dayton twenty-inch bike from Landry's Bike Shop on St. Simons Island, Georgia. NOTE: April 8, 1942 was a dangerous day."

"A dangerous day?" Gracie said. "Why?" Her voice sounded scratchy. Like when she was a parrot in New Jersey.

"You don't need to worry about that," said Grandpa. "Because you're not going. Neither is George." He took off his glasses and rubbed his eyes.

"What about Mom and Dad?" Gracie said.

My stomach did a double somersault. Grandpa didn't mean it. He couldn't. I reached for the paper he held. "Can I see it?"

Grandpa gave it to me.

I looked at the message again. What happened on April 8, 1942?

The word "dangerous" spooked me. But Mom and Dad needed our help. We couldn't go all scaredy-cat on them now.

"Mom and Dad sent us the SOS," Gracie said, still holding her locket. "That means they *want* us to go."

Grandpa shook his head. "I don't know what happened to your parents in Georgia. But I won't risk you getting hurt. Or worse." He put his glasses back on.

His face said *The End*.

That's when I got a great idea. Like always. "All me and Gracie have to do is land on a different day. Right Grandpa?" I said.

"Wrong," said Grandpa. "The time machine decides that. Not you."

Gracie smiled. "So we'll ask it. Real nice."

"It doesn't work like that," Grandpa said. He sighed. "I may need to go this time. Instead of you two."

Gracie grabbed Grandpa's hand. She said, "No, you can't," real loud.

Her voice gave me the heebie-jeebies. Like a zombie walked into the museum. To eat somebody's face off.

Grandpa looked at her with wide eyes. "What's gotten into you, Gracie Stockton?"

"If you get trapped, me and George will be all alone." Gracie's voice was soft now. Like she gets when she cries. I hate it when Gracie cries. It's scarier than when she yells.

She was right, though. Grandpa can never ride in the time machine again. Not ever.

"*We* have to go. Without you, Grandpa," I said. "We can't leave Mom and Dad trapped forever."

Grandpa stared at me and Gracie. Me and Gracie stared at him.

The three of us stood in the middle of the fix-it shop.

Nobody said anything.

taptap tap-tap taptap tap-tap

I jumped. "It's Mom and Dad," I said.

"Oh my goodness." Grandpa grabbed at his pad and pencil. The pencil rolled off his desk onto the floor. He chased after it.

Gracie made for the old telegraph machine.

So did I. But here's the thing: I tripped on my shoelace.

Because it was untied after all.

I landed on the floor.

She stopped walking when I fell. On my stomach.

"Umppff!" I said. Like somebody stepped on a bagpipe.

"I think my gut's broken," I said.

"I think your head's broken," Gracie said. She looked at me. With her hands on her hips. "Maybe you were adopted, George."

"Except we're twins," I said. Duh.

taptap tap-tap taptap tap-tap

"Shhhh," said Grandpa. He scribbled the message on his pad. "George . . . and Gracie . . . Stop . . . Be . . . careful . . . Stop."

Then the machine went quiet.

Me and Gracie didn't move. Gracie's eyes got all watery. Mine did too. I wasn't afraid though. We had been in danger before.

When we traveled to Delaware in 1776.

Pennsylvania in 1903.

New Jersey in 1879. Boy—we got into big trouble in New Jersey.

We got closer to rescuing Mom and Dad each time, though. At least I hoped we did.

I didn't care about danger. I just wanted my parents to come home.

Grandpa put down the pencil. He stared at the message. "We can't leave them there," he said.

I popped up off the floor. "Okay, let's go," I said.

Gracie grabbed my arm. Pulled on me. "Let's get the bicycle," she said.

We ran for the door to the museum.

Grandpa held up both hands. "Hold up there, you two," he said.

Me and Gracie skidded to a stop.

"Ding dang it," I said. He changed his mind fast.

"But Grandpa—" Gracie said.

Grandpa walked toward us. "The bicycle is hanging on the wall," he said. "You'll need help getting it down."

Me and Gracie left the fix-it shop with Grandpa. The time machine sat outside the door. Quiet. An old merry-go-round.

We followed Grandpa through the dark museum. Past the Campbell's Soup exhibit with all the empty cans stacked on top of each other. As high as the ceiling almost. Past the Centuries of Shoes and the Wacky Wigs Women Wore exhibits. Down the dark hallways. Dark except for the green glowing exit signs.

We came to the Round and Round exhibit. Gracie switched on the spotlights. Motorcycles and unicycles and wagons and scooters and anything with wheels made it in here. It's one of my favorite exhibits.

Grandpa lifted a bike off the wall. Shiny red with clean white trim. A bell was clipped on the handlebars. A kids' bike. Super cool times ten.

"The Dayton twenty-incher," Grandpa said. He dropped it to the floor. The tires bounced.

"Can I ride it back to the time machine?" Gracie said. Which was too bad because that's what I wanted to do.

"Hop on," Grandpa said.

So Gracie did. She tore down the hallways. Ringing the bell and screaming "Yeee haaa!" Her screams bounced off the walls.

Me and Grandpa walked fast behind her. Back through the museum.

"At least we know she can ride it," Grandpa said. "That might come in handy on St. Simons Island."

I nodded.

Gracie waited for us outside the fix-it shop. Rode in circles near the merry-go-round.

"Me and the time machine had a talk," she said. She stopped circling. Got off the bike. "I told it we can't land in Georgia on April 8th. I said any other day will be fine. Please."

Grandpa raised his eyebrows. "Did it answer you?"

"Nope," she said. "Doesn't matter. I always get my way."

"I hope so," I said. My stomach swirled like a flushing toilet.

"I hope so too," Grandpa said. He took my hand and squeezed it. "Take care of each other," he said.

Gracie nodded.

"We'll be careful, Grandpa," I said. I squeezed his hand back.

"I'm counting on it," he said. "Let's get this show on the road."

Gracie pressed her lips together. She pushed the bike toward the time machine.

Yellow, green, red, and blue lights came on. Organ music played. Horses and giraffes and tigers and sleds and ostriches and camels went up and down, up and down in a slow circle.

Then ZOOM! the bike flew out of Gracie's hands. It landed on the merry-go-round. Right on top of a giraffe. Now the bike rode round and round. The organ music got louder. The animals circled faster. I felt dizzy watching.

Wind came from I don't know where. It blew hard against us.

"Hurry, kids," Grandpa said. He pulled me forward and took Gracie's hand. He lifted us both onto the merry-go-round.

"Whoa," I said. The floor of the merry-go-round dropped under my feet.

Gracie climbed up on an ostrich. She held on to the pole in front of her.

I stumbled into a sled.

"Don't think about April 8th, George," Gracie said.

Seat belts came out of nowhere. They fastened across our stomachs.

"Okay," I said. *Don't think about April 8th. Don't think about April 8th. Don't . . .*

The time machine went faster and faster. Around and around. The lights lit up the museum outside the fix-it shop. The wind roared in my ears.

We flew past Grandpa. He waved and his mouth moved. I couldn't hear him.

"I don't feel so good," I said to Gracie. She passed me on her ostrich.

Gracie held on to the pole with both hands. Her pigtails flew out behind her.

"Make your mind blank," she said.

I nodded.

Then ZOOM! we were inside a black hole.

CHAPTER 2

It's a Dog's Life

All around me and George and the time machine was black. And cold.

George rode past on the sled.

His hair was awful long. Flowy. Like in a shampoo commercial.

Then THUNK! we were . . . where?

I smelled the ocean. Heard water.

The sun beat down on my face.

I closed my eyes.

I felt like a bobber on a fishing pole. Up down sideways up down sideways. Not such a great feeling after all the round and round on the way here to 1942.

"Gracie?" George said.

Something nuzzled my hand. Cool and wet.

Traveling through time had to get easier. One minute you were being sucked into a black hole, the next you were . . .

What?

What *were* we doing?

"Gracie?" George said again.

His voice was close to my ear.

Something tickled my cheek.

"George?" I said. "It's hot out here and the sun's blinding me. In fact, I might be blind."

I rolled on my side. Opened my eyes. I could see! There was the bike. Gleaming in the sunlight.

And there. So much black hair looked back at me I couldn't speak.

Then, "Bear!" I said. A bear with glasses? "No. Wait. George?"

I leaned closer. That was no bear.

A huge dog looked at me.

Huge.

"Yes, Gracie." The dog's tongue flopped when it spoke.

"George?" I sat up. Grabbed his ears in my hands.

Tipped his head this way and that. "Wow!"

"Watch it, Gracie," George said. Slobber dripped on my pink . . . oh no. I was wearing a dress. Again. With a white tie around the waist. Dang it! Little white socks too. And brown shoes that squeezed my toes.

"Hands off," George said. He licked his lips and nose and chin all in one swipe.

"There are touching rules you know," he said.

"Cool. How'd ya do that, George? How are you making words come out of that huge mouth?" I leaned closer and we tipped to the side.

What? No! George stood on all fours and looked at the water.

"We're in a boat," we said at the same time.

I gripped the wooden sides.

George touched the water with his tongue. "Salt," he said.

"The ocean? Great," I said.

Then I gave George the evil eye. In advance. Just in case.

"Tell me one thing," I said. "Did you think about April 8th?"

"What do you mean?" George said. He looked out over the water.

"George? Did you?" I said.

"Did I what?" Glops of spit landed on the bottom of the boat.

"You did. You thought about April 8th. I bet this is the dangerous day." I grabbed an oar. "We gotta go. We gotta get out of here."

George made a big swallowing sound. "Sorry Gracie," he said.

"Paddle, George," I said.

"Are you mad, Gracie?" George put his head on my shoulder. It weighed a ton. How was he holding that thing up?

Overhead a seagull cried out.

The sun burned down.

I slapped the water with the oars.

"I want to jump," George said. "I feel like I should. Don't you do it, though, Gracie. Not safe for you. But me? I like the water. I can tell."

"Don't you dare," I said. "You had to take swim class *twice*. Even as a dog I bet you can't swim that great."

George looked at me, fast. His ears flopped. I couldn't help myself. I reached out and hugged my brother the dog around the neck.

"You are so cute," I said. "Finally. Don't tell anyone I said so."

"Does that mean you aren't mad?" George said.

"It means it's about time you turned cute," I said. Then rowed again.

"Wait a minute," George said. "What do you mean, dog? I spoke to the time machine too. I said I shouldn't change into an animal again. That *you* should always change shape."

I raised my eyebrows. "I'll discuss that with you later," I said. "Right now we have to get to shore. We're in the ocean, George. And the time machine seems to be this boat we're floating in. It's crowded in here. Me. Huge you. The bike."

He clumped to the front of the dinghy then to the back. He was so big he could only take a few steps. He stepped on me four times. Plus he bumped into the bike. The front tire spun.

"I'm nervous," George said. "Worried. We need to get out of here, Gracie. I love the water. Are you sure I'm a dog?"

He sat long enough to lick his butt then stared up at me. His brown eyes were huge. "What did I just do?" he said. His voice was a whisper.

Ha!

A wave splashed into the boat.

"I'm going to remember that forever," I said.

"What if I start licking people?" George said.

"Not me. Not with that tongue," I said. "Thanks but no thanks."

I looked around. We weren't that far from shore. There were ships out here. Farther out in the ocean. I shaded my eyes.

"*Oklahoma*," I said. "See the words on the side of that one ship? Can you still read, George? And way over there are people on a yacht."

George didn't move. He sighed a huge doggie sigh.

"I wonder if they have a pooch, George," I said.

His tailed thumped once.

Well, well, well.

"At least you are a cute doggie," I said. "Yes you are, George. Yes you are. Good boy!"

George's tailed thumped several times and he sat up.

"This isn't fair," he said. "In this dog suit I can't help but be happy."

I smiled.

"You could have been a girlie poodle," I said. "Dad was."

George tilted his head at me.

"So true," he said.

"Now help me row us in," I said. "The sun is getting lower. It's gonna get dark soon. We have to get rid of this bike."

"Right," George said. He held a paw out to me. "Shake," he said. I shook hands with him.

He peered into the water again.

A breeze blew. Small waves chopped up, slapping at the side of the boat. Already my arms hurt and I had just started rowing.

"You would think this could be easier," I said.

"Never is," George said. Then, "Hey, I saw a fish." He chomped at the ocean.

Even with the waves moving us sort of toward the beach, I couldn't row. In fact, I don't think we moved at all.

A yacht slipped up near us. The name *Bumps* was painted on the side.

"Need help?" a man called.

"Sure do," George said.

"I'll take care of the talking," I said. "Hush."

I cupped my hands around my mouth. I hollered up at the man. "We do. I think we got caught in the tide."

"We got caught in time, you mean," George said. He stood right next to me. He was big enough to ride like a horse. If we were on the shore, I mean.

"Hush," I said. "Sit."

George sat. He looked guilty as a boy *and* as a dog. It was great to see.

"We'll tow you in," the man said.

When we got to the shore, George jumped out of the boat. He ran up and down and up and down the beach. Barking. Like a real, live dog. He was fast.

Way fast.

And big.

Way big.

He ran over to me and put his paws on my shoulders. He was as tall as me.

And super cute.

His being a dog sort of made up for the time he was a rat. Not!

The man docked *Bumps*.

Walked over to where I pulled our boat into the sand.

"Make sure your dinghy gets up good and far," the man said.

"Dinghy?" I said. "You mean him?" I pointed at George. "He's a dog."

"Your boat," the man said.

I knew what he meant. We own a museum, after all.

"The tide might pull it off to sea," he said. "Then what will you do?"

My stomach fell all the way to my feet.

I swallowed hard.

"I don't know," I said. If the time machine floated away, George and I would be in big trouble.

"We need this dinghy to get home," I said.

"You don't want the Germans to get it," the man said.

"Germans?" I said.

"The Germans attacked some tankers off the coast of New York and New Jersey," he said. "Couple of months ago. Used a sub."

The feeling of cold ocean water washed over me.

"Don't worry," he said. "The subs can't see houses on the shore. Long as the people of St. Simons Island keep their drapes shut at night."

"Okay," I said. Even though that's not a good answer to a submarine.

Dangerous day. The dangerous day.

George splashed in the water now.

Here I was working and George was running around like a crazy animal. "George," I yelled. "Get over here and help me move this boat."

But George didn't seem to have doggie hearing.

He kept right on playing.

The yacht man helped me. His face was tan. He smiled a lot. "My name is Charles. Charles Candler." He held out his hand.

"Gracie Stockton." I shook Charles Candler's hand.

"It's good now," he said. "The dinghy's safe. No water will get this craft up here." He looked at me. "What are you doing with the bicycle? I have to admit, I've never seen anyone with a bike in a boat this size. On my yacht, yes. But this, no."

Charles Candler laughed.

I looked at the dinghy. It seemed safe enough. Pulled up on the shore like a few other small boats.

Right near the rocks.

I had to remember where our boat was.

For later.

"Are you all right?" Charles Candler said.

I nodded. Then I said, "We're taking it into town to the bike store. My parents want me and George to drop it off."

"Over on East Beach?"

I nodded. "Sure."

The sun was starting to go down. The breeze turned cool and cooler. I shivered. George barked.

Charles Candler dug around in his pocket. He fished out a coin and handed it to me. "Get yourself a Coca-Cola down to the Five and Dime. Tell them I sent you."

I looked at the quarter. "Thank you," I said.

Charles Candler walked away. "Just head down Main Street," he said over his shoulder.

I pushed the bike toward the road. In the direction Charles Candler said.

CHAPTER 3

Something Smells

"I love running," I said. "Wahoo!"

I plowed through the sand with my ginormous paws. Alongside the wooden dock. It stretched across the beach. Way out into the ocean.

The wind blew the hair out of my face. My slobber blew back too. But who cares about that? I could run like this all day.

Until Gracie told me not to. Which she did.

"Stop, George," Gracie said. "Stay."

She came toward me. Pushing the bike through the sand with both hands. She grunted.

"Ding dang it," she said.

I don't know why I obeyed her. But I couldn't help it. I stopped. Sat down. Panted for air. My tongue hung out of my mouth.

Every little sound made my ears twitch. No matter how far away.

I could smell even more stuff.

Like salt. Wet tree bark. Fish. Not like fish sticks. The alive kind. That swim around in the water. I got a whiff of ham sandwich. My stomach growled.

Cars parked on the beach. People walked by the water. I sniffed the air for that ham sandwich.

Then I remembered . . . me and Gracie didn't know what day it was.

A lady sat on a blanket close by. Reading a book. A man slept in a chair next to her.

"Do you know what day it is?" I said. *Oops!*

"Why yes," the lady said. She kept on reading. "It's the seventh."

"Arf," I said. I don't know why.

The lady looked up. Her mouth dropped open.

"Abner, Abner," she said. She shook the man. "Wake up. That dog talked to me."

"Sure he did, Gladys," the man said. His eyes didn't even open.

"And he's wearing glasses."

"Right, Gladys. Right." The man covered his face with his straw hat.

I bounced away. Over to Gracie. "Guess what day it is?" I said. I plopped my paws on her shoulders. Looked her straight in the eyes. Again. Which was great because she's taller than me. When I'm not a dog.

She stopped. A sweat drop inched down her forehead. Onto her eyebrow. The right one.

"Stop doing that." She pushed at me. "Just tell me, George," she said.

"Somebody's grumpy," I said. I jumped down. "April 7th. Not April 8th. So we're okay. We need to give the bike back today. Then get home."

"And maybe find Mom and Dad," Gracie said. "I really want to see them again."

"Me too," I said. "But we have to hurry."

"Hurry?" Gracie wiped her face with the back of her hand. "Can you push the bike faster than me?"

"Arf, arf," came out of my mouth. Like a drum going BOOM BOOM.

What the heck? This barking stuff was crazy.

The wind blew Gracie's dress against her knees. Her pigtails ruffled like feathers.

"Does that mean yes?" she said. But her face said *Real funny, George.*

"Maybe," I said because what do I know? I don't speak Dog.

I sat down and scratched myself. Turns out that sand itches.

Gracie looked past me. So I looked too.

The lady named Gladys watched us. With binoculars.

"Umh," Gracie said. "We should leave, George."

So Gracie pushed the bike up the hill. I zig-zagged around her. Clear up to the road.

Wow! I could see the island now. Bushes and trees and stuff grew everywhere. That made me pant and pant. I loved trees all of a sudden. I wanted to run over there and go potty. On. Every. Single. One.

Across the road a lighthouse almost touched the sky. It stood near some other buildings. Fat palm trees grew around them.

Gracie looked at the sky. "The sun's going down, George. We have to hurry."

The wind changed. It blew in my face. I sniffed.

The hair on my back stood up. I never thought evil could have a smell.

Until now.

"Gracie, something smells weird," I said. "Maybe Crowe is close by. My doggie sense is going crazy."

Gracie stared at me. "What doggie sense, George?"

"Mine. It's like a super power," I said.

"Whatever," she said.

A cat jumped out of a bush. Across the road. It saw me.

I saw it.

"Arfarfarfarfarfarf," I said and bolted.

"No, George," Gracie said. Her voice sounded like a smack on the nose. So I stopped.

The cat ran back into the bushes.

"Yeah, real evil, George," Gracie said. She hopped on the bike. "Here's *my* super power."

She stepped down hard on the pedals. "I'll race you to the bike shop."

She peddled fast. But I could keep up. Easy peasy lemon squeezy.

"Yee-haw!" Gracie yelled into the wind. "Run, George, run," she said.

"Arf, arf," I said. I meant it too.

We raced past some houses. They sat way back in the trees. Away from the road.

Gracie's legs went pumppumppumppump-pumppumppump.

I ran like pa-dump. Pa-dump. Down the road. Because my long legs could reach out a mile.

A blue car passed us with its top down. The woman driving wore sunglasses. The scarf on her neck blew straight back. She smiled and waved.

"Arf, arf," I said.

"I like this bike, George," Gracie said. "I wish we didn't have to give it back."

She leaned forward. Pumped the pedals faster.

I ran alongside her. Up the curvy dirt road. Into St. Simons Village. Toward Landry's Bike Shop.

If we could find it.

We coasted into town and slowed down.

Boy was I thirsty. I looked for a pop machine. Or a water fountain. Or a puddle.

All I saw were shops on both sides of the street. Lots of people walking in and out of them. Talking and carrying bags and packages.

Gracie stopped the bike. "Are those soldiers, George?" she said, pointing.

Three guys sat outside at a table. They wore uniforms. They ate . . . sniff . . . fried fish. And . . . sniff . . . French fries. My slobber dripped like a leaky faucet. "Yeah. World War II is going on, you know." I couldn't take my eyes off that food. "I'm hungry, Gracie."

"First we give this back," Gracie said. "Then we can eat." She pushed the bike along the street. We walked up one side then down the other.

"Let's ask somebody where the bike shop is," Gracie said.

She stopped in front of a man sitting on a bench. Reading a newspaper. He held it in front of his face. Fishing poles leaned inside the shop window behind him.

"Excuse me?" Gracie said to the man.

He didn't move.

I found a shady spot to lie down. Georgia is a hot place. My insides felt like a volcano. I panted and panted. It didn't cool me off.

Another man knelt in front of me. He patted my head. "Poor fellow," he said. "How about some water?"

It was the guy who helped us pull our dinghy onto the beach. I sat up and whined. My tail thump thumped on the ground.

Gracie glanced at me. I couldn't help the whining. Or the tail. This dog thing was a mystery.

"Hello, Mr. Candler," Gracie said. She walked her bike to the sidewalk. Closer to me and Charles Candler.

"Hello Gracie," he said. "Call me Charles. And you're George." He scratched my ears. "You look hot, buddy. It's all that dark fur."

I whined some more. Thump thump. I looked at Charles's glass. Then at him. Then the glass. No way would I say one word though. No matter how thirsty I got. Not after the lady on the beach with the binoculars.

Charles set his water glass in front of me. Like he could speak Dog or something. I lapped it up with my huge tongue. It splashed all over my face. The ground. My paws. It tasted so good. I was his best friend after that.

"I didn't know you were *that* thirsty," Gracie said. She petted my head. With one finger. "Sorry, George. You stink."

I didn't care. I sucked up the rest of the water.

"Did you get yourself a Coca-Cola?" Charles said to Gracie.

One of the guys in uniform laughed. "Can't even give away that drink of yours, Candler?"

"What does he mean?" Gracie asked.

Charles Candler shrugged. "My family made Coca-Cola," he said.

"You mean, your family owns it?" Gracie said.

He smiled. "We used to," he said.

Whoa. Charles must have a gazillion dollars. Plus all the pop he could drink.

"Arf," I said. My tongue was dry as cotton again.

Gracie put her hand on my head. Like *Hold on, George.*

"Cool," she said. "I love Coke."

"It's best cold," Charles said.

"Arf," I said. Because we had to get going.

Gracie looked at me.

"Can you show us . . . I mean, me, where that bicycle shop is, Charles?" Gracie said. "Landry's? I need to find it fast."

"Oh. Fast," said Charles, grinning. "That sounds like a real emergency."

Gracie turned red. I rolled over and wiggled around on my back. I had an itch.

"That's on South Island," he said. "You sure you want to go that far? It's a ways off. And there's a nice bicycle shop right here on East Beach."

"It has to be Landry's," Gracie said. She crossed her arms. Her lips tightened up.

Charles didn't say anything. He looked at Gracie.

I whined again.

Now Gracie whined. Better than me. "Please, Mr. Candler. We have to go today," she said. "Even if it's ten miles away. Before it's too late."

"All right, Gracie," Charles said. He put his hands up. "If it's that important to you." He pointed. "Landry's shop is off Ocean Boulevard. On Peachtree. But you'd better hurry."

Gracie hopped on the bike. "Thanks, Charles," she said. "Come on, George." She rode away down the street.

I ran after her.

Charles shouted, "See you around."

When I looked back, the man on the bench with the newspaper stood up.

He lifted his head. His eyes shined. Like gray light bulbs. Mean ones.

I caught up to Gracie. "Crowe is here," I said.

Gracie peeked back over her shoulder.

"He heard us talking to Charles," I said. "He knows where we're going."

"We have to get there before he does," said Gracie.

Crowe watched me and Gracie ride away.

We raced in the direction Charles said to go. He wasn't kidding either. Landry's was a long way off. We rode down Ocean Boulevard. Close to the beach.

A couple of kids walked along the sand toward the water. They held fishing poles.

Cars whizzed around us.

We flew down the road. I could smell the ocean in the wind. Wished I could jump in.

I had a hard time keeping up with Gracie. She rode as fast as a fire engine. Except she didn't have a siren.

After a thousand years Gracie turned onto Peachtree Street. "There it is, George," she said.

I followed close.

Gracie put on the brakes. She jumped off the bike in front of Landry's Bike Shop.

"Ding dang it," Gracie said. She shaded her eyes with one hand. "Ding dang it."

I gulped when I saw the sign on the door.

GONE FISHING. BACK TOMORROW.

Tomorrow would be too late.

CHAPTER 4

Crowe Crowe Crowe!

"Closed?"

My hands were sweaty on the handlebars. The bike leaned sideways a little. For a minute I wasn't sure I could hold it up.

A salty breeze blew down the street. My dress wrapped around my knees with the wind.

George sniffed his way to the door. He jumped up on the glass. He had to be the biggest dog in the world.

"Gone fishing," he said. He plopped onto all fours. "That's what the sign says."

"I see that, George," I said.

George sat. He scratched behind his ears. His glasses went crooked. Then they fell back into place.

"Think I got fleas?" he said. "I better not have fleas."

"What are we going to do, George?" I said. "We gotta get this show on the road."

Grandpa always says that. I missed him.

I put the kickstand down.

Made my hands into fists.

Marched to that door with the handwritten sign.

"Gracie," George said. "You look like you're about to . . ."

I pounded the door. "Open up," I said. I pounded on the door again. The glass rattled. "We got something for you, mister. A bike. Hey, mister!"

A man came out of the shop next door.

"Ain't there," he said. He wore a long apron.

I wanted to say "No duh." But instead I didn't say anything.

"Gone fishing," he said.

I glanced at the apron man.

"Always going fishing."

He disappeared into his store.

I touched my locket for good luck.

Then I pounded on the door again. Both fists. If there was anyone here, I would make sure they heard me. Even if they *had* gone fishing.

George growled. A deep growl. A scary growl.

"Hello, George. Gracie."

I spun around. Crowe stood on the sidewalk. He rested a hand on the bike.

How did he get here so fast? My skin got prickles.

"Go away," I said.

"Is this it?" Crowe asked. "Is this the time machine?"

George barked like crazy then. He ended with, "We'll never tell you where the time machine is." Then he was barking again.

"Never," I said.

I turned back to the door. But my knees shook. Cupping my hands around my face, I peered through the glass. There was a row of bikes. All arranged according to color. Plus there was a place for one halfway down the aisle.

"I see where the bike goes," I said. I acted like Crowe wasn't standing so close. George still growled.

He came up next to me. On all fours he was as tall as my belly button.

"Crowe," he said. His voice sounded . . . well, doggie. "I'm gonna take a chunk out of your leg."

"I'm here to help, George and Gracie," Crowe said.

"We don't need your help," I said.

The time machine was stashed on the beach. Safe. As long as we didn't tell Crowe what the time machine looked like, I mean.

And I wasn't saying nothin'.

If we could stay away from Crowe this trip, me and George would be fine.

I tapped on the glass one last time.

"See, George," I said. "Right there. That empty place." I jiggled the doorknob. Nope, the store really was locked. "I bet that's where this bike was parked."

"I could bust through the window," George said. "I'm pretty strong now."

I looked at him. Put my hands on my hips. Thought about it.

"You probably could," I said.

"Want to see my muscles?" George said. He grinned at me. No matter what anyone says to you, dogs can smile. Even dogs who are your brother.

"You better not break anything, George," I said.

"We might get in trouble with time."

If there is anything we've learned, it's you can't mess with time.

George licked his lips. Slobber went everywhere. As a dog, George had more slobber than the average boy.

"Children," Crowe said. He stood closer to us now.

I could see him in the reflection of the glass. He held his hat in his hands.

George growled again.

"Children," Crowe said. "Let's work together. I keep telling you that."

"Crowe," George said. He let out a bark then spoke again. "We won't work with you. Mom and Dad told us not to trust you. They said that before we went to Dover. And we don't. We never will."

"The time machine is mine," Crowe said. He sort of smiled. "You both know that."

I swallowed. I remembered meeting Mr. Edison in New Jersey. Crowe and Edison had worked on the machine together.

We stood in the shade of the building. I shivered even though it was warm outside. Shadows from the buildings fell across the road. Before we knew it, it would be night.

Then what?

The dangerous day.

Tomorrow was the dangerous day.

"The time machine is not yours," I said. I caught George by the ear and gave him a gentle tug. "You stole it from Mr. Edison. And you stole more things. Let's go, George."

But where?

I looked around.

An old man and woman, old as Grandpa, walked toward us. They held hands.

A bunch of kids talked in the street. They looked the same age as me and George. They each had an ice cream cone.

What were we supposed to do now?

"Let's go," I said again. I still had hold of his ear. George's hair was soft.

"That ice cream sure looks good," George said, slobbering.

"I can make it easier for you, Gracie," Crowe said. He put his hat back on. "You won't be alone. We can figure this out together."

But me and George didn't even look at Crowe.

We walked to the bicycle.

My heart thumped.

Every time. Every time it happened like this. We got to the place to return the stuff Mom and Dad bought for the museum. Then Crowe showed up. To stop us. To steal from us, if we let him.

Where were they? Where were Mom and Dad?

I looked around the street.

I didn't want to be alone.

But I didn't want to be with Crowe, either.

I wanted Mom. I wanted Dad.

"It's going to be dark soon," Crowe said. "I've

been here before. I know a place you can stay."

Did he know what I was thinking?

Or did he just understand what it was like to be in a strange city?

"Come, George," I said, whispering.

Down the street we walked. I pushed the bike. George trotted along, head to the ground. Then he wagged his tail like crazy. He ran ahead sniffing.

Crowe came up next to me. He was tall. Taller than my dad. Way taller than Grandpa. Way way taller than George the Dog.

Now Crowe talked about us teaming up together. Me and George and him. But I didn't answer.

I looked at the blue, blue sky. Growing darker.

Looked at the paved street.

Glanced over at the Five and Dime store. A poster said *Buy War Bonds.*

Crowe didn't know where the time-machine-turned-into-a-dinghy was.

Yet.

We were safe.

For now.

George ran around the corner ahead.

"Don't go too far," I called. "George."

"Gracie," Crowe said. "You know me." He pressed his hands to his chest.

A family walked out of a store ahead. A mom. A dad. A boy. A girl. They all held hands.

Like Mom and Dad and me and George had two years before. Before our parents got trapped in time.

"You know I want to go home too," Crowe said.

"I'm busy," I said. The bike clicked as the wheels spun. I climbed up on the seat.

"We want the same thing," Crowe said.

I stared him in the eye.

"No we don't!" My voice was quavery. And a little loud. "I want my parents. You want the time machine. If you get it, me and George might not get home to Grandpa. We'll never see Mom and Dad again."

Then I pedaled away. The way George had gone.

"Gracie," Crowe called. His voice exploded in the quiet air. "Gracie, I am going to get you. And George. And that time machine. You know I will. You can run. But I will always be there."

My hands shook.

Crowe was dangerous. He would leave us here forever. If he got the chance. But I couldn't think that.

Instead, I thought about getting away.

And about Landry's storeowner.

Who would go fishing in the late afternoon?

Why?

George barked.

I stood to pedal.

The bike wobbled. I straightened it out.

When I came around the corner, George sat right next to a girl with a fishing pole. A girl our age.

She had one hand on George's head.

I braked. Got off the bike.

"You know this dog, Miss?" the girl said.

I nodded.

"I do," I said. "His name is George."

Her hair was braided.

She wore a dress like mine and she smelled like . . .

"This *your* dog, Miss?" she said.

"Miss?" I said.

The girl sort of looked at me.

I sort of looked back.

"Why's he wearing glasses?" she said.

"He doesn't see so great," I said.

She nodded.

We stood there. Quiet. Sort of looking at each other.

George panted and smiled. And panted some more.

"I'm Gracie," I said. Then I stuck my hand out to her.

She stared at me hard.

Real hard.

Then shook my hand.

"Hey Miss Gracie," she said.

I shook my head. "Just plain Gracie," I said.

George grinned.

"I'm Linda," the girl said. "Been fishing."

Everybody on St. Simons Island must fish.

Linda held up a line with four fish strung through the gills. All had sand on their eyes. And long whiskers. Their gills still moved.

"That's like the bike my uncle sold last week, Miss Gracie," Linda said. "He owns Landry's. I was there when the man bought the bike. Why do you have it?"

Linda sounded like a detective.

"Ummm," I said. "Just call me Gracie."

"I like your dog," Linda said. "I had a dog. Violet. Ran away."

I nodded. Opened my mouth to say something.

"You visiting the island?" Linda said. "Staying at one of the beach houses? I live over that away. Want me to walk with you? Are you lost? Come on. I can help." She didn't wait for an answer. "Come on, boy," she said to George.

George nodded at me.

I knew, just like that, we were giving this bike away tonight.

Maybe even going home before the sun sunk clean away.

CHAPTER 5

Big Chicken

I trotted along beside Linda. Her bare feet were covered in sand. Up to her ankles. She dragged the fish behind her. Catfish.

Cats and fish. Two of my favorite things nowadays. I could chase one and eat the other. My slobber glands kicked into high gear.

Linda talked and talked and talked. "When Momma has her baby I'll be Big Sis. I'm hoping for a girl. How about you, Miss Gracie? Got any sisters? Or brothers?"

It looked to me like Linda didn't want to let go of that "Miss Gracie" stuff.

Even with Gracie giving her the look.

"One brother," Gracie said.

"Baby brother?" Linda said.

"Sometimes," Gracie said. She gave me a *so there* face.

I growled.

"What's wrong, George?" Linda said. "Miss your boy?" She ruffled my head.

I sniffed Linda. She smelled like fish. And something else yummy.

We walked along on the trail by the water. The trees nearby were thick. I thought about running into them and lying in the shade. All this fur heated me up like an electric blanket.

Linda didn't stop talking for one second. Me and Gracie couldn't get a word in edgewise. She never even took a breath. I don't think.

"Ya'll don't talk much," Linda said.

I stared back at Gracie. She pushed the bike on the sandy trail. The tires bumped over ruts and clumps of grass. She kept looking over her shoulder.

"Crowe?" she said.

I sniffed. Nope. I couldn't smell him. Or see him. For sure he was somewhere close by, though.

I could feel his eyes on us. Waiting for his chance to steal me and Gracie and the time machine. To take us back to his time. In 1879.

Sniff. Grape fish.

That's what Linda smelled like. I licked her hand. The one not holding the fish line and the fishing pole.

"Stop that, George," Gracie said. She rang the bike bell at me. "It's rude to lick people without asking first."

"Ah, he's all right, Miss Gracie," Linda said. She pulled a purple ball out of her pocket. "He's sniffed out a treat. Here you go, boy," she said.

She shoved the ball into my mouth.

Candy! Grape flavored. CRUNCH. With bubble gum in the center. I chewed and chewed.

"Don't get that stuck in your fur," Gracie said. "I'll have to give you a buzz cut." She snorted. "You'll be naked."

"Nah. He'll swallow it," Linda said. "That's what my dog used to do. It'll come out his back end later tonight."

Gracie busted out laughing. She stopped the bike in the road. Then bent over and laughed some more.

I barked and jumped up on her. Chewed my gum right in her face. "Arf," I said. Hearing her laugh made me all happy inside.

Gracie pushed me. "Down, George," she said. But she didn't stop laughing.

I couldn't help jumping on her. Like her laugh was a hamburger or something.

Linda cocked her head. Hitched the fishing pole over one shoulder. She watched us. "I'm going home. Where're ya'll headed, Miss Gracie?"

"Nowhere special," Gracie said. "Sit, George, sit."

I sat. And worked on blowing a bubble.

"Don't you do it, George," she said. She had a bad-dog warning in her eyes. I whined. I would make a little tiny bubble. Later. When Gracie wasn't looking.

Linda scratched me behind my ears. That was getting to be my favorite thing in the whole world. I leaned toward her.

"That's a good dog, George," she said. "I like him."

I smiled. Gracie raised one eyebrow at me like *Don't get used to it, George.*

We walked some more. Along the water. Away from town.

I saw maybe three houses on the road. People sat outside on their porches. Talking to each other and fanning their faces.

Linda waved and said, "Hey, how ya'll doing?" to everybody.

"Does your uncle Landry live close to you?" Gracie asked.

Clever Gracie. If her Uncle Landry lived nearby, we could stop at his house. Drop off the bike. And race off to our dinghy time machine. Bing Bang Boom. We're outta here.

"Nah," Linda said. She tossed a rock into the trees. "He's on the other side of the island. If he's home from crabbing yet."

"Ding dang it," I said.

"Quiet, George," said Gracie. She looked up at the sky. "Brother," she said.

Linda stopped.

She bent down. Put her hands on my face. Her nose on my nose.

"Don't pay any attention to his noises," Gracie said.

I rolled my eyes up at Gracie and whined. She scrunched her face. Like *Now you've done it.*

"Hmmm," said Linda. She took my glasses off and spit on them. Then she wiped them with the hem of her dress.

"George is a smart dog," she said. She put my glasses back on me. Her face came into focus.

She walked on ahead. Humming.

"A lucky dog, you mean," said Gracie. She pushed the bike past me.

"Sorry Gracie," I said. Quiet so Linda couldn't hear. "I keep forgetting I'm not me."

"Yeah, I know. You're a dog, George," she said. "A crazy one. You gotta help me. So stop goofing around and talking out loud to people. We'll never get home if you don't."

I felt bad. I sort of liked being a dog. Instead of the brains of the family.

"I'll try to concentrate, Gracie," I said. I meant it.

Until Linda said, "Fetch, George," and threw a stick into the trees.

I took off. Running after that stick was fun fun fun. All I could think about was getting it.

Then a nasty little gray squirrel screamed at me from high up in a tree.

I forgot all about the stick. And jumped up on the tree trunk. "Arfarfarfarfarfarf," I said back. I never wanted to get a squirrel so bad before.

"Oh, George," said Gracie. "Come on."

I ignored her. "Arfarfarfarfarfarf."

"George." This time Gracie dingdingdinged the bike bell.

I looked at her.

Then up at the squirrel.

Dingdingding.

I trotted back to the trail. I felt sorry for goofing around again. But I couldn't help it. That dumb squirrel.

Gracie sighed. "Let's go, George," she said.

She sounded worried. I needed to be George the boy from now on. Brains of the family. For Gracie and Mom and Dad. Not George the dumb dog. If I could.

Linda stopped in front of a white house a ways down the trail. "This is where I live," she said.

The house had a blue screen door. Flowerpots sat in a line on the porch. A woman knelt in the dirt in the yard. She planted flowers. Pink and purple and yellow and white ones. She had dark hair. She wore a dress and an apron. Plus she would be having a baby soon.

"Hey, Linda girl," the woman said. She looked up. Brushed the hair off her face. She was pretty too. Like Mom. "Who's that with you?"

Sniff. I smelled chicken. And sausage. And . . . bacon. Oh my gosh BACON.

"Hey Momma," Linda said. "This is Miss Gracie"—she nodded to Gracie—"and the big hairy one slobbering all over the place is George."

Linda's mom nodded at us. "Miss Gracie," she said.

Miss Gracie? Again? I looked at Gracie. She didn't look like a Miss to me. I couldn't figure out why everybody kept saying that.

"Can . . . they stay to supper, Momma?" Linda said. Her face was like *PUH-LEASE*?

Gracie looked straight down at the ground. She kicked the dirt. Her cheeks went pink like the flowers.

I didn't feel shy because I was s-t-a-r-v-i-n-g. Plus I was a good beggar. I trotted over to Linda's mom. Sat down. Licked her arm. "Arf," I said. Which was supposed to mean *I like you. I like bacon.*

Linda's mom wiped her arm with her garden glove. Smoothed the hair on my head. Then she gave Linda a strange look.

"I'm sure Miss Gracie's folks are expecting her home."

"Naw," Linda said. "They followed me here. Like they don't have a place to go."

"You hush, girl," Linda's mom said. Her words were sharp.

"Yes'm," Linda said.

"You visiting St. Simons?" Linda's mom said.

"Arf, arf," I said because Gracie didn't answer.

I nudged her with my nose.

Linda's mom smiled at Gracie. "I'm talking to you, honey. Not your dog. Where're you staying?"

"Um . . ." Gracie said. The pink turned red. "We don't know yet. I'm hoping to go home tonight. I have to give this bike back to Mr. Landry first. But his shop is closed."

Linda glanced up at her mom like *See? I told you.*

I looked from Linda to Linda's mom to Gracie. Gracie didn't look at anybody. Just dug into the dirt with her shoe.

Linda's mom said, "I think we can help with that, Miss Gracie. After I get you something to eat. Why don't ya'll go on inside and set the table. Get washed up. Supper's in an hour. We're eating late tonight. Waiting for your daddy, Linda."

I loped up the steps and stood at the door. I couldn't pull it open. So I whined. Which is hard to do when you're working on a bubble gum bubble.

"You can put your bike by the back door," Linda said. "No one's going to steal it. This is a respectable neighborhood. What's your daddy do? My daddy's with the Merchant Marines. You know? The soldiers that drive those big oil tankers out on the ocean."

Linda went on talking as she walked Gracie to the backyard. Gracie pushed the bike and nodded. She didn't say anything.

I couldn't figure out why she was being so quiet all of a sudden.

I waited at the front door until Linda opened it from inside. Then I trotted on in. Like I owned the place.

Linda's mom followed me. "That's some dog you've got there, Miss Gracie," she said. "Huge but real polite. And smart."

"He's okay," Gracie said. "Thanks for letting us stay, Mrs.—"

"Call me Maybelline," Linda's mom said.

"And I'm just Gracie," Gracie said.

"Arfarf," I said. Which meant *Nobody calls her Miss Gracie thank you very much.* "You're more than welcome, M—Gracie," Maybelline said.

I pricked up my ears at the sound of a car engine. And tires crunching on sticks and sand.

A door slammed. Someone ran up the front steps.

Did Crowe follow us here?

A man charged through the front door.

I jumped at him and barked. But he wasn't Crowe.

"Whoa," the man said. "Who's this?"

I wagged my tail. He scratched behind my ears. "Who put the glasses on him?"

Linda ran at the man. "That's George, Daddy," she said. "He doesn't see too great."

The man opened his arms and caught Linda in them. He laughed. "How's my girl?" he said.

Then he set her down and crossed the living room in two long steps. Kissed Maybelline on the lips.

"We have company, Lonnie," Maybelline said. "This is Gracie. She's visiting with Linda. I was hoping we could give her a ride to your brother's house. To drop off a bike." Maybelline smiled.

Gracie gave her a little smile. She held on tight to a handful of my neck fur.

Lonnie nodded. "Miss Gracie," he said.

"Just Gracie, Daddy," Linda said. She grinned at Gracie.

Lonnie's eyebrows went up. He looked at Maybelline. "Is that so?" Lonnie said.

"Yes," Gracie said.

"Well, then." He ran his hand over his hair. "I think we can take a drive to Hugh's. After dinner. I am starved. So you call this bear George, eh?" He winked at Gracie.

Bear? Was I that big? I looked around for a mirror.

Gracie blushed pink again and held my fur tighter.

"Go on, Daddy," Linda said. "You know he's a dog."

"Arf," I said, which was supposed to mean *Yep*.

Lonnie had a giant laugh that he used a lot. Like when I licked him after he petted me. "You're just a big teddy bear, aren't you? A big baby bear," Lonnie said. Then he wrestled with me and Linda until dinner.

Gracie watched us. She sat on the couch with her arms folded over her stomach. Stiff as a door. She shook her head when I whined at her to play.

After a while Maybelline called from the kitchen. "Come and eat," she said.

Everyone sat around the table. Maybelline set a big pot in the middle. She gave me my own bowl for dinner. On the floor next to Gracie. I got bacon and some chunks of sausage. I never liked sausage before. But now. Oh boy.

Maybelline spooned food into everyone's bowl.

"Pass that cornbread this way, sister," said Lonnie. He pointed to a plate piled high with yellow muffins. "And some of that fried catfish my girl caught today."

Linda grinned. She scooted the plate over.

My nose couldn't make out all the smells in my dish. Corn. Tomatoes. Onions. Fish something. I licked a little. BAM! That stuff was better than Mr. Hershey's chocolate. I slurped up every last bit.

Gracie stared into her bowl. So did I.

"You never tasted gumbo before?" Linda said. She shoved a spoonful into her mouth.

"No," Gracie said. "What is it?"

"It's my favorite, that's what," said Linda. "Taste it."

"Leave her alone," said Maybelline. "She'll come to it in her own time."

Lonnie and Maybelline ate but they watched Gracie.

"Go on," said Linda real quiet.

I whined and pushed at Gracie's arm with my nose.

She put a spoonful of gumbo in her mouth.

Nobody made a sound.

"Wow," said Gracie. "That's good."

Maybelline smiled big.

Linda said, "See? I told you."

"I miss your good cooking at sea," Lonnie said.

He took another bowlful from the pot. "I'm on an oil tanker," he said. "The *SS Oklahoma*."

Then he told us stories. About being a Merchant Marine.

"*SS Oklahoma*?" Gracie said. She swallowed a tiny bite of muffin. Glanced at me.

I opened my mouth. Then shut it. That huge ship we saw when we first landed in the ocean.

"Yes," Lonnie said. "We call it a Liberty Ship. It carries oil to where it's needed. Without oil, our planes and ships and submarines and tanks won't run, will they now?" He ate the catfish in two bites.

"Arf," I said.

"That's right, boy," Lonnie said to me. He tossed cornbread under the table. For me. I scooted closer. Waited for more.

"Merchant Marines have a serious job to do here at home," Lonnie said.

Maybelline took his bowl. "More, Lon?" she said.

He kissed her cheek. "You read my mind, honey."

Linda ate more than I did. I couldn't believe it.

"Pass the tea, please Momma," she said.

Her tummy made her shirt pooch out. She watched her dad tell his funny stories. Laughed crumbs of muffin all over the floor.

No problem. I sucked them right up like a vacuum.

Gracie still didn't say much though. She didn't eat all that much, either. Just little bites, here and there.

Maybe she was mad at me for playing around too much.

Lonnie got serious after dinner. "I don't want you to worry, honey. But we're hearing stories of another German submarine nosing around. Captain thinks it's the same one that sunk those tankers up the coast a few months back."

My doggie sense kicked in then. For reals. I had a bad feeling. Not the hungry feeling like usual.

I put my head on Gracie's knee. She looked at me with wide eyes.

Maybelline's smile drooped. "What?" she said in a small voice.

Linda stopped gathering up our plates. "But it won't come here, right Daddy?" Linda said. "Not to St. Simons?"

"Don't worry, little girl," Lonnie said. "Your daddy will keep you safe."

He squeezed Maybelline's hand.

Lonnie looked worried. Like Grandpa when me and Gracie leave in the time machine.

Gracie put her hand on my head. "We gotta get home, George," she said.

I licked her hand. I had to think of something.

CHAPTER 6

First K-I-S-S

Seeing Linda's mom made me lonesome for Mom.

It felt like a fish bone stuck in my throat.

Maybelline petted Linda's hair. Used her own spit to wipe dirt off Linda's cheek. Kissed Linda on the forehead.

Just like Mom did with me and George. My mom. Before she left.

That darned fish bone got bigger and bigger.

And Linda's dad. Her dad reminded me of *my* dad. How he used to laugh when George did something dumb.

Being here on St. Simons Island was like being home with Mom and Dad.

But not.

'Cause we weren't at home. And we weren't with our mom and dad.

When Lonnie said a prayer on the food, he held Linda's hand.

"Thank you," I said. My voice came out all squeaky.

"Whatever for, Gracie?" Maybelline said.

"For dinner," I said.

I wanted to say for being like my mom and dad. But I couldn't.

Lonnie smiled. He dished out the peach cobbler for dessert. He gave me a piece from the middle.

Even when Linda said, "Hey, I wanted that one."

Maybelline said, "Manners, Linda."

"Yes ma'am," Linda said. She looked at me. "You can have the best part, Gracie."

George barked.

"Gracie," Lonnie said. "We can get that bike over to my brother's place soon. Sound good?"

I would have said "Yes sir," except for that fish bone.

Instead, I nodded.

George trotted around the table. He grabbed my dress in his teeth. He pulled.

"What, George?" I said.

George growled at me.

I looked around the table. "My dog needs me," I said. My voice was back.

"You may be excused," said Maybelline.

Then she smiled. Just like Mom would have.

I ran outside through the living room. I went onto the porch. Sat in a rocker. George was right behind me.

"Gracie," he said. He put his feet into my lap. Put his hairy face close to mine. "What's the matter?"

I swallowed.

Spanish moss hung from all the trees. It looked like old lady hair. I could smell the flowers Maybelline had planted. Mosquitos buzzed.

"I want to hurry," I said. "Get back to the museum."

My face felt hot.

George breathed on me. He had sausage breath.

"So do I," George said.

"Linda has her parents," I said. "I want mine. I want ours."

George sniffed around my neck. "We're working as hard as we can," he said. "Right, Gracie?"

I didn't answer.

"Mom and Dad bought a lot of stuff from the past," George said. "We've got a lot of work to do. It's gonna take a while."

"I know," I said, whispering.

"Be brave, Gracie," George said. He looked at me with those doggie eyes. "If you aren't brave, maybe I can't be either."

I breathed in deep. Squeezed my hands tight.

My brother was a smart dog.

I could do this.

"You're right, George," I said. I stood up. The rocker hit me in the back of the knees.

"What did you say?" George said. He tipped his big head at me.

"You heard me," I said.

"Excuse me, Gracie?" he said.

I lifted his ear. "You're. Right," I said.

"It's about time," George said. He grinned.

"Stop that," I said. "You look like a boy stuck in a dog suit."

George wagged his tail. "As you know," George said, "this is the real thing."

"George, Gracie?" Linda called.

I heard Lonnie walking through the house. His footsteps echoed on the wooden floor.

Maybelline was singing. "I'll be seeing you," she sang. "In all the old familiar places."

Seeing who? Mom and Dad? I hoped so.

And not Crowe. I glanced around the dark yard. Was Crowe out there? I knew he was. Where?

Could he see me and George? Would he get us?

Lonnie pushed open the door. Stepped out on the porch. Stretched so I thought he might touch the ceiling high above.

"Gracie," Lonnie said. "I had Maybelline cover your supper for later."

"Thank you," I said.

George trotted up to Lonnie. He scratched around my doggie brother's collar. Adjusted George's glasses for him. His tongue hung out. George's. Not Lonnie's.

"Let's get that bike back to my brother's place. What do you think?" Lonnie said.

"I think, great!" I said. And I meant it.

I hurried off the porch to the bike.

Looking for Crowe.

Thinking about Mom. And Dad.

Maybelline and Linda came outside. George wove between their legs.

"You're not a cat, George," I said.

He looked at me. Made his eyes go wide. Scrunched up his nose.

"He's fine, Gracie," Linda said. She squatted. Grabbed George by the ears. Then she planted a kiss right on his face.

"Ha! George," I said. "Your very first kiss."

Linda put her hands on her hips. "I always kiss dogs. Even when Momma says I can get ringworm."

"Oh," I said.

George barked once. But I noticed he didn't come over by me. Nope, George stayed with pretty Linda. Who might get ringworm from kissing him.

Ha again!

I wheeled the bike to Lonnie's car.

"Cool," I said. "Backwards doors on the car."

Lonnie tipped his head a little. "I wish it would stay cool. Days are warming up. Nights can be nice. Well, we're headed for summer. If this war doesn't stop us." He patted the bicycle. "Let's tie that contraption to the bumper."

George ran to me.

He was panting when he jumped up. He put his paws on my shoulders.

"Did you see it?" he said.

"Move a little, George," I said. "Can't push the bike."

"Did you?" George was whispering.

"Do you mean Crowe?" I stopped.

Looked around.

"No," George said. "Did you see the car?"

"Yes." I sort of dragged the bike. George took doggie steps backwards. I looked over his shoulder. "It's blue," I said.

"A Buick," he said. Then he was gone. Running. Running fast. This way and that. George had to be the happiest dog on the planet. And boy too. George the boy loves cars.

"What got into him?" Maybelline said.

"He likes to ride in the car," I said.

Me and Linda helped Lonnie tie the bike to the bumper.

George ran. Everywhere. Around the yard. Up on the porch steps. Back to the car where he ran three circles around it.

A breeze blew past. I could smell the ocean.

My brother barked like crazy. Kicking up sand as he went.

Lonnie laughed.

Linda let out a whoop.

We climbed in the car. George stuck his head right out the window. Slobber dripped everywhere.

"Gross, George," I said. "Plus don't get hair all over everything."

"Violet got hair all over everything," Linda said.

"We didn't care."

George raised his eyebrows at me.

Being a dog, I could see, was the life. Horses, rats, birds. They all had good things about them. Well, maybe not the rat. But a dog? Everyone loves a dog.

"Just a little farther," Maybelline said.

We drove to Mr. Landry's house.

There was a blue star on the front window.

"Let's go, George," I said.

"I'll help," said Lonnie.

"Me too," Linda said.

We untied the bike. I pushed it to the house. It was small and white. Red shutters were at each window. A man and woman sat in the living room.

"We're dropping off a bicycle," Lonnie said through the front window. "Hugh, get out here."

The man hurried to the door. He looked like a younger version of Lonnie. With more hair. "*The Shadow* is on the radio," he said. "You know I don't like to be interrupted during that program."

"Going home," Lonnie said, "right after this delivery."

Lonnie looked at me.

So did Hugh Landry.

For a long time.

"I have to give this bike back," I said. I wheeled it to the front steps. Put down the kickstand.

"What? I just sold that thing not too long ago," Mr. Landry said.

"I know," I said.

"But why?" Mr. Landry said. "Didn't the man like it?" Mr. Landry paused. "I knew it wouldn't work for him."

George sat quiet at my knee.

"Why not?" I said.

"Oddest thing. He carried a bowl with a goldfish in it," Mr. Landry said. "I asked him if he wanted a bike with a basket. He said no."

Mom, a fish? In a bowl?

George barked. It sounded just like a laugh.

"George," I said. "This isn't funny."

But Mom as a fish *was* funny.

"Did he want the basket after all, Miss?" Mr. Landry said.

"No sir," I said. "We just don't need it anymore."

"You have him come to the store tomorrow and I'll be sure to give him the money back," Mr. Landry said. He leaned the bike against the house.

"Sure," I said. "Okay."

I glanced at George.

We wouldn't be coming back tomorrow. We had to go home. Tonight.

"Hugh," said the woman inside. "You're missing the program."

Linda jumped up and down.

"Hey," she said. "You heard from Mikey?"

Mr. Landry shook his head. He put his hand on Linda's shoulder. "You will be the first to know."

Linda threw her arms around Mr. Landry's waist. "Promise?" she said.

"Promise," he said.

"Let's get going," Lonnie said. "Don't want car lights showing the enemy where we are. And I have to get back to the ship."

We climbed in the car.

George's ears went up. His eyes said *Enemy?*

"I wish you didn't have to go back tonight," Maybelline said.

"No need to worry," Lonnie said.

"I do worry," Maybelline said.

"Me too," Linda said. She looked at me. "My daddy helps protect the country. So does my cousin, Mikey."

Lonnie glanced over his shoulder.

George had his head out the window.

"Lots of Americans are working for the war effort," Lonnie said. "I do my bit."

"He's my hero," Linda said. "We pray every night my daddy's safe. 'Cause our boys are dying in this war."

"Hush, Linda," Maybelline said.

"They are, Momma," Linda said.

We were out of the trees now. Linda pointed at a home where the curtains were drawn. There was a gold star on the front window.

George put his head on my lap.

"That's Tommy Jones's house," Linda said. "He died. They put the gold star in the window. Blue star means they're fighting. Yellow means they were killed."

"I said, hush, Linda," Maybelline said.

"His sister is my friend from school," Linda said. "And now he's gone. Forever." Just like that, Linda started crying.

And even though we had taken the bike back for Mom and Dad, I didn't feel happy. Not at all.

CHAPTER 7

A Dangerous Day

When Lonnie drove the car into the dirt driveway I whined. No way did I want the ride to be over. Not yet.

Lonnie turned off the car. The lights went out.

"Home sweet home," Lonnie said. "I gotta shove off in a couple of hours." He put his arm around Maybelline. "How about we all sit out on the porch for a bit?"

"I'll pour us some tea," said Maybelline. "Come on, girls."

Lonnie and Maybelline got out of the car. They walked up to the porch. Holding hands.

Georgia got real dark all of a sudden. And creepy. Buzzing and slithering noises came from outside. Wings flapped. I lay on the back seat and put my paws over my ears.

Me and Gracie would never find the dinghy now. We'd have to wait until morning to go home.

Gulp. Tomorrow was April 8th. The dangerous day.

Plus we didn't have anywhere to go tonight.

Crowe was waiting for us. Somewhere. In the dark.

Bad. Bad. Triple bad.

The crickets outside chirped loud.

"Can you stay a while longer?" Linda said. She opened the car door and climbed out. "I'll sure miss having a dog around when you go." She ruffled my fur and walked toward the house.

I whined because I would miss her too.

I put my paw on Gracie's shoulder. "Fat chance finding the dinghy," I said. "Which means we can't get home until tomorrow. *Tomorrow*, Gracie."

My tummy itched like crazy. Out of nervousness. Or because I needed a bath. I scratched it with my back leg.

"Where are we going to sleep tonight?" said Gracie. "We need one of your big ideas. Right now, George."

"How about we hide out in the woods? It'd be like camping," I said. I like camping. In our own backyard. On the trampoline. In a sleeping bag.

"With the snakes, you mean?" Gracie said. "And the spiders? And the lizards?"

She stared out the car window. Right when Linda stuck her head inside.

Gracie screamed.

I jumped into the front seat.

That girl was everywhere.

"It's just me," Linda said.

I peered over the front seat. "Whoa. Did you hear me, I mean, us? Talking?" I said.

"George," Gracie said.

Oops.

"Sorry," I said.

Oops again.

That's when Gracie choked. She couldn't stop.

Linda smacked her on the back. "You okay?" she said.

Gracie shook her head. She wadded the front of her dress. "Are you going to tell?" she said.

"Naw," said Linda. "It's no big deal. Violet talked to me all the time." She grinned. "She sure was a funny old dog."

Gracie blinked. And blinked.

Until I said, "Rude, Gracie."

"Can you stay awhile longer? Momma tells great ghost stories."

"Maybe we can sleep over?" I said. "But I have to have a pillow."

Linda scrunched her face up. "Y'all want to stay at our house? Overnight?"

Gracie frowned at me. "Rude, George. We can't sleep over. We have to get to the beach. Tonight. It's important."

Linda twisted her mouth. She said, "Hmmm," and rested her arms on the car door. "I got an idea. How brave are y'all?"

"Not very," I said.

"Very," said Gracie. "What's your plan?"

"Okay, here's what we do," said Linda. "You pretend to go home. After Momma's ghost stories. I let you into my room through the window. Then when Momma is asleep, we sneak out with my daddy's flashlight. We can get to the beach in something like twenty minutes."

I swallowed hard. Sneaking in and sneaking out. In the dark. With all the creepy crawlies coming after us. Too freaky for me.

What would happen if we stayed on St. Simons until morning, though?

Gracie didn't say anything. She wadded her dress some more. "Okay," she said. Her voice sounded froggy. "We'll do it."

Linda opened Gracie's door. "Let's go then," she said.

Her parents sat in the porch swing. They held glasses.

Maybelline leaned back with her legs crossed. "This baby can't come too soon for my poor back," she said. A pitcher of tea sat on the table beside her.

I licked my lips and scooted closer.

Linda leaned on Lonnie's shoulder. "Can Gracie and George stay for a while longer, Daddy?"

Maybelline sipped on her straw. She looked at Gracie. "What about your folks?"

"They're . . . out of town. We're staying with our grandpa," Gracie said. She chewed her lip.

It wasn't a lie. Mom and Dad are out of town. Way out.

"He won't mind," Gracie said. "But I can call him later. After he gets home."

That part was an almost lie. We couldn't call Grandpa. Boy did I wish we could.

"Where is he?" Maybelline never took her eyes off Gracie. Like she was thinking over what Gracie said.

Linda looked at Maybelline. Then at Gracie.

Lonnie sucked on his straw. Watched us all.

"He works real late most nights. As a fix-it man," Gracie said.

That was true too. Gracie was good at leaving out the important parts of the story. Like how we got here in a time machine. And how Grandpa is waiting for us . . . in the future.

"These two would be good company for you and Linda, May," Lonnie said. "What do you say?"

Maybelline uncrossed her legs. She sat forward in the swing.

"I think it's a fine idea," she said. "This girl needs looking after. With that hard working granddad of hers gone to all hours." Her eyes got all shiny. "We can tell ghost stories. What do you say, Baby?"

Linda nodded hard. "Yes ma'am."

"Why don't you go on in and clear up the dishes now?"

"I can help," Gracie said. She stopped beside Maybelline's chair. "Thank you," she said so quiet I almost didn't hear.

Maybelline squeezed her hand. "You're welcome, child."

I put my paw on Maybelline's lap and looked up at her. She said, "You're welcome, too, George."

Linda and Gracie went inside. I stayed on the porch. Begging for tea.

"Isn't that cute?" said Maybelline. "I wonder if George can drink out of a straw?"

I made a yelp which meant *Yes, and I will show you.* I scooted closer.

"Now, honey," said Lonnie. "Don't tease him."

"Okay, then," said Maybelline. She poured a glass. Set it down in front of me. "There you go, boy."

I sucked up that tea. Right through the straw.

Maybelline laughed and clapped. Lonnie said, "That's a good boy."

Lonnie stood and held out his hands to Maybelline. "It's about that time, May. Drive me to the dock?"

"If you can get me outta this thing," she said. "I feel like an elephant."

Lonnie pulled her up from the swing. "Light as a feather," he said.

"Oh, go on," said Maybelline. She hugged Lonnie.

Watching them together made me feel like hot cocoa all over. Warm and sweet. "Arf," I said. Lucky Linda.

Maybelline called through the screen door. "Linda? I'm taking your daddy to the dock. Come and say goodbye."

Lonnie patted my head. "Watch my girls tonight, buddy," he said.

Linda ran onto the porch. She pushed the door open. It banged against the house. "Bye, Daddy," she said and jumped on Lonnie. Sort of like I jump on everybody.

He hugged her tight. "Be good for your momma," he said.

"Yes, Daddy," Linda said. She hugged him back. "You be careful."

He set her down. "You know I will. Look for me in a few days. When we get back from delivering fuel to New York City," he said. He walked down the steps with Maybelline. Holding her hand.

Gracie didn't come out with Linda. I peered through the screen.

Lonnie started the car and drove down the road. Linda sat on the steps. I sat next to her. She was quiet. Which was weird for Linda. I put my paw on her leg.

"I'm okay, George," she said. "Just worried about Daddy."

The buzzing chirping slithering sounds seemed even louder now. I saw tiny white lights flying around in the dark trees. I crowded up next to Linda.

"What're y'all doing?" Gracie said. She stood behind us.

"Y'all?" I said. Then "Oops."

Gracie shook her head. She twisted her mouth to the side.

Linda laughed. "Gracie's fitting in real nice around here."

When Maybelline got back, we went in the house. "To start the party," Linda said.

They didn't have a television. Maybelline turned on the radio. We listened to these guys named Abbott and Costello. They were so funny. Linda and Gracie yelled "Hey, A-bbott!" over and over.

Then Linda played records. Like the ones we have in the museum. And we danced around the living room. Maybelline made popcorn in a pan on the stove.

When it was almost midnight Maybelline said, "I hope your granddaddy won't be worried about you, Gracie."

Gracie shook her head. "He won't be home yet."

"Then I guess we have time for ghost stories," Maybelline said. Her voice went all spooky.

The crickets got loud outside. I looked out the window. I saw something move. I think. Gulp.

We brought pillows and blankets into the living room. I dragged in a fluffy pillow by my teeth. Maybelline turned out the lights. She eased onto the floor with us. And lit a candle. The wind blew the flame. Shadows walked along the walls.

I squeezed up next to Gracie. "Fraidy cat," she said.

"Tell Boo Hag, Momma," said Linda. She pulled

her blanket to her chin. She looked at Gracie with big, round eyes.

Gracie sort of smiled. Held her locket tight.

"Good idea," said Maybelline. "That's a true one." The candle made her eyes glow. Which made my stomach get all wiggly.

We huddled up while she told a story about a boy named William.

"He fell in love with a beautiful girl who lived in the swamp," Maybelline said.

Gracie put her arm around my neck.

"So they got married. But every night, William's bride would stay up. Knitting. Until William fell asleep."

Maybelline's voice was low. She rested her hand on her baby tummy.

"One night, William only pretended to fall asleep. His beautiful bride disappeared into the attic. William followed her. He watched from a dark corner. And what he saw scared him half to death."

I crawled under Gracie's blanket and whined. I love ghost stories. Most of the time. Georgia was a dark, spooky place already. So Maybelline's story freaked me out.

"Right before his eyes, William's bride slipped out of her skin. She had become a Boo Hag. A terrible monster. William gasped when he saw what she was. And when she heard him, she jerked around and . . . AHHHHH!"

Maybelline grabbed Linda.

Linda screamed.

Then Gracie screamed.

Then I screamed. Like a dog.

Maybelline laughed and laughed. "That one gets you every time, baby girl," she said to Linda.

Linda had the blanket over her head. "I know, Momma," she said. "It's my favorite."

"Can I use your bathroom?" Gracie said.

Maybelline nodded.

"Come with me, George," said Gracie. She still had a hold of her locket.

I crawled over and lay in Linda's lap. Looked up at Gracie. No way was I going down that dark hall.

Gracie ran to the bathroom. She turned on the light. Slammed the door behind her.

Maybelline yawned. "It's way past my bedtime," she said.

Linda pulled the blanket off her head. She nodded. And winked at me.

"Okay, then," said Maybelline. She crawled to the sofa and pulled herself up. "I'll get ready for bed. Check on y'all in a bit." She walked out of the room.

"Okay, Momma," said Linda.

Gracie ran back in. Jumped under her blanket. "That story scared me to pieces," she said.

"It's after midnight," Linda said in a whisper. "You all go on outside. Then come around to my window. After Momma's asleep"—she held up a flashlight—"we'll sneak out."

Gracie stared right into the flashlight. Lucky for her it wasn't turned on. Otherwise, she'd be blind. That's a true story *my* mom told *me*.

Me and Gracie hurried out the front door. We took off around the corner of the house. To Linda's window. Before the Boo Hag could get us.

"Get off my feet," Gracie said. Because I was right up next to her. She felt her way along the outside wall. "Linda," she whispered.

I heard the creak of a window sliding up.

"Over here," she said. Just ahead a light jumped up and down in the dark.

I looked all around. I could feel the bony fingers of the Boo Hag on me. Something buzzed my ears. "Aahhh!" I yelled.

"Shhh, George," said Linda. She leaned out her window and waved. "Come on."

Gracie climbed in.

I jumped in.

And hid under Linda's bed.

"Momma fell asleep in her room. But we gotta wait. In case she wakes up and peeks in on me."

Gracie and Linda sat on her bed. Linda made a light show on the ceiling with the flashlight.

I fell asleep and dreamed the Boo Hag flew into the room. She smashed all the windows with a giant hammer.

I woke up barking.

KA-BOOM.

The house shook like a meteor slammed into it.

Then I saw the broken glass all over the floor.

Another KA-BOOM shook the house.

I barkbarkbarkbarkbarked.

Which meant *What. In. The. Heck?*

Linda and Gracie screamed.

CHAPTER 8

Stowaways

I sat straight up. Where was I? When had me and George gone to sleep?

My heart pounded so hard it felt like a fist in my chest.

"What?" I said. I sort of screamed the word. "What was that?"

George howled. He ran at me. Fast. Knocked me onto my back. My elbow hit the wooden floor.

"Help," he said. The word was a bark too. "My ears. My ears, Gracie."

Another boom and there was the sound of more glass shattering. For a moment I couldn't hear anything. And then screaming.

George wailed again.

Jumped on me.

"What's going on?" he said.

"I don't know," I said. I wrapped my arms around George's neck. He was trembling.

So was I.

Mom. Dad. Were they here? Did they know what was going on now? It was April 8, 1942.

The dangerous day.

More screams came from down the hall.

Maybelline hurried into the room. She snapped on lights. Tied on her housecoat. She looked like she had seen a ghost.

"Gracie?" she said when she saw me.

Linda ran right to her mother. "Momma what was that? What blew up?"

Then Maybelline said, "Lonnie. Lonnie."

Her voice was a wail.

"What's happened?" I said. I still couldn't hear so great. George ran around the room, barking. We went into the living room. The windows were broken in here too. The world around us came alive. I could see lights on in the houses nearby.

People screamed.

Called out to one another. But I couldn't understand what anyone said.

"The explosion came from the beach," Maybelline said.

"Daddy!" Now Linda cried. She tried to put her arms around her mother.

But Maybelline ran down the hall. Linda followed. So did me and George.

Maybelline went out the front door. In her housecoat. Her feet were bare. Then she was back.

She threw off her housecoat as she ran. I could see her nightgown. Lace at the sleeves. She hurried to her bedroom.

Linda followed her mother. "What is it?" she kept saying. "Tell me, Momma."

Maybelline didn't say anything.

George butted my hand with his nose.

"This is the day, Gracie," he said.

"I told you not to think it," I said. My heart still slammed in my chest. "When we were in the time machine, I said, 'Don't think about April 8th.'"

"I didn't mean to," George said.

Linda's crying voice filled the living room.

George sat down, then tipped his head to the ceiling and howled.

Someone ran past outside. Banged on the screened-in porch door.

"Going to the beach, Maybelline," a man called. "Something's been hit. It may have been the *Oklahoma*."

Maybelline was in the living room. Her blue pants and pink shirt looked too pretty for now. For a time when we were all so scared. So scared George wouldn't stop howling. So scared I might throw up.

Thank goodness I hadn't eaten too much dinner.

Linda grabbed hold of her mom's hand.

"What about Daddy?" she said. "What about Daddy?"

Maybelline turned and knelt in front of her daughter. For some reason I wanted to cry. I missed my mom kneeling in front of me. Touching my hair the way Maybelline touched Linda's now. And I was terrified.

I wanted Lonnie here with my friend.

I wanted her father home. Safe.

I wanted Mom and Dad back home.

"Your daddy is fine," Maybelline said. Her voice was shaky. "Your daddy is just fine."

Maybelline stood. She grabbed a scarf from the table and tied it around her hair.

"Then why are you going?" Linda said. "Take me with you. Let me come."

Outside there was more yelling.

I heard someone scream, "John! John!"

George ran to the window and looked out. He ran back to me. Brushed up against my leg.

I wrapped my arms around his neck.

Maybelline held Linda by the shoulders.

Her voice was soft.

"You three stay here," she said. "Where it's safe. Today is a dangerous day."

"I could help," Linda said. "I want to help."

I let go of George. My legs wanted to give out.

"Me too," I said. "I could help too."

George was over to Maybelline before she could stand. He licked Maybelline.

"George, too, Momma." Linda helped her mom up. "George could help. Violet would have."

"Stay home," Maybelline said. "Wait for me here. Go to bed, if you can. Sleep. I'll be back before you know it."

Then Maybelline ran from the room.

I heard the screen door slam shut.

Linda covered her face with her hands.

"It's okay, Linda," I said.

When Linda looked up, I knew.

"I'm going," she said.

"Right," I said. I straightened my dress. Retied the belt. "I'm going with you."

"Me too," George said. He let his tongue hang out.

Barked.

In less than five minutes, we were outside.

It was dark except for people's house lights. And flashlights.

The air was damp and cool. Smelled like the sea.

We ran out to the road.

Sand slipped in my shoes. But I kept going. Jogging next to Linda. George running ahead a little. Coming back to us. Running ahead.

Every once in a while a car zoomed past us.

Then the world would go dark.

Linda and I held hands. Her palm was sweaty. I knew she was crying. I was crying too. But she never slowed.

"How do you know where to go?" I said.

"Me and Daddy come out here lots late at night," Linda said. "To go shrimping off the pier."

I swallowed.

"My dad and I fished together," I said. "When he was home."

George barked from somewhere up ahead.

"I miss him," I said.

We ran on.

Until we were at the shore.

People were everywhere. Running to the dock. Standing in the surf. Getting in small boats with engines and roaring away.

There was no engine on our dinghy.

I looked to see if I could see it in the dark.

There was just the shape.

Then I looked out at the water.

I couldn't move.

Far out at sea I saw fire.

Fire on the water.

How?

Linda was really crying now. "Daddy's ship," she said.

George ran up to us. The moon reflected on the sand. On the waves. Little stars pricked the sky. His glasses reflected the fire on the water.

Yellow smoke clouds rose into the night sky.

"We'll save him," George said. "We'll save your dad. Come this way. I found a boat."

I ran through the sand. I fell once. Linda pulled me to my feet.

If I had to, I would row our dinghy into the ocean.

The waves crashed on the shore.

I heard a woman saying something about bombs.

Someone else said submarines.

"I need more hands on deck," a man called.

At the end of the pier was a huge boat.

"That way," George said. "We're going to that boat." He ran ahead of us.

"That's *Bumps*, Charles Candler's yacht," Linda said.

We ran down the pier to the water. The yacht was being untied.

Charles stood at the top of *Bumps*. Like he was on top of the world. How would I ever make the jump? The yacht seemed to grow as I looked at it.

Gulp.

He cupped his hands around his mouth.

The wind blew. His jacket rippled.

"Pushing off," Charles said.

"Let me on board," another man yelled.

"Uncle Hugh," Linda said. "Take me with you."

He turned. "Go home, Linda," Mr. Landry said. "Take your friend . . ." He glanced at George. "Your friends with you." Then he was on the boat.

"Keep still," George said. He crouched low to the pier. "Wait till I tell you."

"I gotta help my daddy," Linda said. She called after her uncle. Mr. Landry didn't look back.

"George has an idea," I said. "Don't worry, Linda. His ideas are always good. Sometimes."

Charles rushed down steps and then down more steps until he was in the belly of the boat.

"Get ready," George said. "We're gonna jump."

There were a few lights on *Bumps*. But mostly it was dark.

The waves slapped at the pier. At the yacht. The engine grew louder.

Men hurried everywhere on the boat.

Two women on the pier cried.

"Now," George said with a bark. He jumped. Linda didn't even wait. She jumped too. Below me the water was dark as black paint.

"Stop that little girl," someone said behind me.

I looked over my shoulder. Crowe!

I stumbled.

"Gracie," George called.

"Come on, Gracie." Linda's voice was screechy.

I closed my eyes. My knees shook. I might not make it. I might not.

I jumped.

Landed on the lip of the moving yacht. I teetered. Swung my arms for balance. "Whoa!" I said.

George grabbed the hem of my dress in his teeth. Linda clutched my hand. I tipped back toward the water.

But they held me safe.

"This way," George said. "A place to hide." He sniffed his way to a dark corner.

We all crouched in the shadows.

Listened as *Bumps'* engine revved.

Then we zoomed through the water.

We watched as the fire grew bigger.

We moved closer and closer.

To where the water seemed to burn. Smoke billowed. The sky of stars was covered. Sometimes the moon was hidden. The air smelled burnt.

"What are you doing on board?" an older man said.

How had he found us?

"No women or children." He looked at George. "Or dogs. This is a dangerous mission."

"That's my daddy's oil tanker," Linda said.

Then we heard screaming.

Men screaming.

Calling for help.

The water burned.

George paced. He ran to the edge of the yacht.

He barked and barked.

"Gracie," he yelled. "I'm going. I can see them. They're drowning."

I ran to my brother. Took ahold of his collar.

"You have to stay with me," I said. "George, you can't go out there."

"Gracie!" George looked right at me. Licked my face and I didn't even care.

I wrapped my arms around his neck. "Please stay with me," I whispered. "Please don't go. I'm scared."

George shook free. "I have to, Gracie."

Then he leaped into the dark water below.

CHAPTER 9

Dog Paddle Rescue

I did a belly flop. Right into the ocean. It felt like landing on the sidewalk.

I never could get diving down. Even though Mom showed me a thousand times. She would tell me, "Arms up, George," and stand next to me on the edge of the pool. "Point them at the water. Like an arrow."

My stomach always hit first.

I wish Mom could see me now. I still couldn't dive. But I could swim like crazy.

I dog paddled to the surface. I wished I had windshield wipers for my glasses. To clean off the drops of water.

All around me was a white glow. Like someone had turned on the lights. I saw the big ship all lit up with fire. *SS Oklahoma* was painted on the side. Lonnie's ship.

Some of the men swam away from the fires. Some just floated. They didn't move.

Were they even alive?

I panted and paddled in place. I am not brave like Gracie. I didn't know what to do.

"I wish Mom and Dad were here," I said.

"Help. Over here," somebody yelled.

The water smelled like gasoline. Smoke got in my nose. Burned my eyes. My throat.

I gagged and almost threw up.

More voices yelled for help. All around me.

A man waved his arm in the air. He choked and spit. His face was burned and bleeding.

"Come here, boy," he said to me in a quiet voice. He kept closing his eyes and slipping under the water.

I had to help him. Even though I didn't know how.

I swam to him as hard as I could.

When I got close he grabbed a handful of my hair.

His face told me he was scared.

So was I.

I whined. Because that's what dogs do when they're freaked out. I think.

"Am I glad to see you," the man said.

"Arf," I said. Then I paddled paddled paddled as fast as I could. Away from the fire.

The man was heavy. I had a hard time pulling him. But he kicked his feet. That helped a lot.

"Good boy, good boy," he said. He kept saying it in a quiet voice. All the way back to *Bumps*.

The ocean was so dark. What if a shark was sneaking around here? I got a shiver.

Then a bright light swept over us.

Someone yelled out, "Man in the water." Two men in life jackets jumped out of the yacht. They grabbed the man.

"There's a dog in the water too, you know," I said. To myself though.

Linda and Gracie stood on the deck. Gracie stared down at me. Her face was red and blotchy. Like crying blotchy.

"What took you so long, George?" she said.

"Did you see my dad out there?" Linda said. Her voice choked. She held Gracie's hand.

"No," I said. "But I'll go back. I'll find him." I dog paddled in a circle.

"Get in this boat right now, George Stockton," Gracie said. Like she's the boss of me. Which she is not.

"I can't," I said. "There are more guys out there. I have to save them, Gracie."

"No, George," Gracie said. Her voice got loud. "You'll drown." She squeezed her locket. Her eyes went wide. "Remember what happened in swim class?"

Charles stepped up behind Gracie. "You put your dog in swim class?" he said.

"Um . . . yeah," she said. "He's sort of . . . slow. For a dog."

"Arf," I said. I'd show her who's slow. I paddled back into the dark. Toward the men in the water.

Gracie screamed after me. "George."

"Arf," I said again, which meant *I'll be all right, Gracie.* I hoped I would be anyway.

Bumps started with a roar. It slid along beside me.

A lifesaver dropped in the water.

"Get on, George," said Gracie. "We'll give you a ride." She leaned over the rail. "Please."

I climbed on the lifesaver. Because Gracie looked more scared than I felt.

Charles pulled me onto the boat. "Welcome aboard, George," he said. "We can use your sharp eyes. This smoke is thick as cream." He peered into the night through binoculars. "That enemy sub might still be out there."

"Enemy sub?" Gracie said.

"A Nazi sub did this to my dad's ship?" said Linda. She clenched her fists. Clamped her jaws tight.

"That's what they're telling me on the radio," Charles said.

"I hate them," said Linda. Tears rolled out of her eyes.

Gracie hugged Linda's arm. "Don't worry," she said. "Charles will find your dad."

I put a paw on Linda's stomach. And yelped. Which meant *Me too*.

Then I shook and sprayed water all over the place. Couldn't help it.

"Whoa," Charles said. He backed away.

"Oh my gosh, George," Gracie said. She put her hands over her face. "Rude."

Linda hid behind Gracie.

They looked like they got soaked by a fire hose.

That. Is. A. Cool. Trick. I couldn't wait to show Grandpa when we got back home.

Bumps slowed down.

That's when I heard it again. The voices from out on the water. Calling for help.

The men on the yacht leaned over the side. Watching. Watching.

"Shine the light on the surface," said Charles.

But the smoke was too bad and the light couldn't get through it. The fires were spreading in the spilled oil. Rescue boats roared all around us.

"Can't see," one of the crew said. "We've got to get closer. Or we'll never find them in time."

I could see the men. I could hear them too. Calling for help.

Linda ran to the edge of the yacht. "Daddy?" she said. "Where are you?" She screamed. "Daddy Daddy Daddy!"

That's when I heard Lonnie. With my super dog hearing.

"Don't be scared, Gracie," I said. "I'll be right back." I jumped into the water. On my belly again. *Ouch.* I paddled toward Lonnie's voice.

Gracie yelled for me to stop. But I couldn't. I had to save Lonnie. For Linda and Maybelline. For their new baby.

Splash Splash Splash Splash Splash.

Men from the yacht jumped into the water after me. They had on life jackets.

"Follow George," said Charles.

I smiled. Sort of. Like a dog does. Because now I was like those Navy guys on TV. The ones that jump out of helicopters into the ocean. To save people.

The spotlight followed us. We swam through the smoke. Through the oil.

Men yelled for help. They floated in the water on pieces of wood and stuff. One by one the crew pulled them back to the yacht.

Except for Lonnie.

He was far away from the others. He tried to hold another guy up. But they both disappeared under the water. Then they came up again. Lonnie coughed.

Lonnie called to me when I got close. His face was shiny from the oil.

"George," he said. "Where did you come from, buddy?" The man Lonnie held had blood on his forehead. It ran down his face. He didn't open his eyes.

"I could kiss you right now," Lonnie said.

"Arf," I said. Which meant *I am glad to see you too but please don't kiss me.*

I didn't feel scared this time. Not too bad anyway. I knew what to do.

I paddled up next to Lonnie. He threw his arm around my neck. And turned the other man on his back. "Okay, let's get out of this death trap," he said.

I swam back toward the light from *Bumps*. Lonnie and his friend were harder to pull than the first guy. But I was strong. Like a superhero rescue dog.

The light pointed right on us. Then Splash Splash Splash three men jumped in the water. They swam to us. Grabbed Lonnie and his hurt friend.

I was so glad to see them because my legs were tired from paddling.

Linda hugged Lonnie and cried when he got on board *Bumps*. He hugged her back. "It's okay, sis," he said. He cried too.

The crew wrapped blankets around the men from the *Liberty*. Gave them hot drinks.

"Let's get these guys home," said Charles. *Bumps* sped back toward the lights blinking on the shore. "Keep your eyes sharp for that sub."

That made my legs shaky. I sat on the deck. Black oil covered my fur. It stunk like crazy.

Gracie squeezed my neck so tight I couldn't breathe. "You're in so much trouble, George," she said. She squeezed tighter.

"Gracie . . . I . . . can't . . . breathe," I said.

She let go. Wiped her eyes. "I'm telling Grandpa when we get home," she said.

"Me too," I said. Boy would I.

CHAPTER 10

I'm Okay, You're Okay

All night the fire burned.

The ship burned. Even as it sank.

I watched the *Oklahoma* as we hurried back to the shore. Lonnie needed help. Needed to go see a doctor. So did the other men.

Some of them were burned. Some of them cried out. Others didn't say anything.

George stood beside me. We looked over the railing.

"Maybe I missed some of them," George said.

I wrapped my arm around his neck. He was wet. And smelled stinky. Just like he sometimes does when he's a boy.

"Missed some what?" I said. But I knew what he meant.

"Some of the men," George said.

His voice was trembly. I could feel his heart pounding.

"You did great, George," I said. "You were so brave."

I buried my face in his neck.

Lonnie could have died. If George hadn't been there. If we hadn't come on this dangerous day.

"You saved Linda's dad," I said.

George licked my face. Licked the tears away.

"I'm okay, Gracie," George said.

Bumps rumbled beneath my feet. Waves crashed into it. The salt water splashed on me. I shivered. Far from us now, the ship burned. Lights swept the water.

Other boats kept searching for more of the *SS Oklahoma*'s crew.

"If we keep going back in time, we'll get Mom and Dad. Right, George?" I said.

"Right," he said.

I kissed the top of my doggie brother's head.

Then leaned on the railing.

Overhead the moon was covered by clouds. Or smoke.

This was the scariest time travel of all.

The saddest one of all.

Men lay around us. Everywhere on the deck.

We pulled next to the pier. *Bumps* hadn't even stopped moving. People from the dock climbed onto the boat.

"George. Gracie." It was Linda. She came up to us. "Daddy says he's okay. He thinks he can go home."

We got off the yacht.

Walked down the pier. A breeze filled with smoke blew past us. I heard the water splashing on the boat.

Down to the beach we went. Waves lapped at the shoreline. The night seemed even darker than before. Darker than when we had come here a few hours earlier.

"Linda?" Maybelline said. She rushed forward. "I've been looking for you everywhere." She grabbed Linda up close. "Where have you been?"

"I had to rescue Daddy," Linda said. She spoke right into her mother's tummy. Lonnie came forward. Hugged Maybelline.

"You're safe," Maybelline said when she saw him. She threw her arms around Lonnie. "I was so worried."

Then she looked at me and George and Linda.

"I cannot believe you three went out there," Maybelline said. "That's very naughty."

"Now, May," Lonnie said. "Don't be too mad. George found me and Thomas. Pulled us to help. I'm not sure I would have made it without the dog. For sure I couldn't have saved Thomas."

They hugged again. And in all the celebrating I saw Crowe.

Watching us. He stepped forward.

I backed up. Right into Linda. I even stepped on her foot.

George barked.

"That was a dangerous trick, George and Gracie," Crowe said. "You put the time machine at risk when you do things like that. You put us *all* at risk."

He turned and walked away.

"Time machine?" Lonnie looked at me and George. "What's that crazy man talking about?"

But we didn't have a chance to answer.

More boats came ashore. Charles called for more volunteers.

That's when I saw Dad.

Carrying the fishbowl. Mom swam around in it.

They were on the yacht. With the new group of people. Getting ready to go help, maybe.

Dad looked at me over the railing. He blew a kiss. And waved.

"George," I said. "It's Mom and Dad."

George ran. Down the dock. He barked like crazy. I thought he might leap into the water.

But he didn't.

Bumps pulled away.

Mom and Dad were gone.

George came back. It was hard to see him in the night. He blended in with the darkness.

"They left," he said. "Again."

I knelt and wrapped my arms around his neck.

"I miss them," I whispered into his ear.

"Me too," George said.

"Let's go, Gracie," Maybelline said.

I didn't want to.

But I was so tired I almost couldn't stand.

So me and George and Linda and Maybelline and Lonnie all walked toward their house. The sand was hard to step through. Mosquitoes buzzed. I heard frogs crying for rain.

George brushed up against me. "Is the dinghy where we left it?" He spoke in a whisper.

"Yes," I said. "Right there by the sand dunes. Near the rocks."

"As soon as the sun comes up we go, okay?" George yawned big. As he was trotting along. It was almost cute.

"Good idea." I looked around. "Do you see Crowe?" I said.

George didn't even answer. Just shook his head. And yawned again. "Don't smell him either," George said.

The walk seemed to take forever.

Then we were there.

The lights in the house were still on.

"We've got to pull the shades," Lonnie said. "When I'm on the ship, I can see the lights from the houses."

We climbed up the stairs. Onto the porch. My legs were so tired. Lonnie went inside.

He was covered in oil.

He still dripped water.

His shirt was torn and I could see both arms looked bloody.

My stomach turned over.

George was already asleep. In an oily puddle on the floor.

"You're hurt," Maybelline said. "Lonnie."

He flipped off all the lights we had left on.

"I'll be okay," Lonnie said. He scooped Linda and Maybelline up close. "I'll be okay," he said again.

I watched them hug. Looked at my brother, the dog, sleeping on the floor. Wished for Mom and Dad.

Even if my mother was a fish.

If I could hug them both one more time.

Maybelline said, "We have to get to help, Lonnie."

He straightened up. Ran his hand through his hair. "I'm okay, Maybelline. I just need a bath. Then I can see to these wounds."

Maybelline smiled.

"No," she said. "*I* need the midwife. The baby is coming."

"What?" I said it and Lonnie said it and Linda said it. All together.

George looked up at us. He cocked his head to one side. His tail thump thumped. Then he rested his head on his paws and went back to sleep.

"Let's go to my sister's, seeing we have company," Maybelline said.

"Me and George can leave," I said.

"I wouldn't think of it, Gracie," Lonnie said.

Maybelline went to her room. She came out with a bag. "Ready," she said.

Lonnie helped her out the front door. "You girls stay right here," he said over his shoulder. "No going out for anything. You hear me?"

Linda nodded. So did I.

"Keep the drapes closed." He shut the door behind him.

"I want a sister," Linda said long after her mom and dad left.

Me and Linda were in her bed. George was curled up on the rug right next to me.

"A brother isn't so bad," I said.

I whispered because dogs can hear pretty good. Maybe even when they're sleeping. Some things a brother doesn't have to know.

My eyes closed.

I guess I fell asleep.

When I woke Lonnie and Maybelline were still gone.

Linda was sleeping.

George stared at me, paws on the bed. Slobber dripping onto my neck. He stunk.

"Yuck," I said. "Back off, George."

Sun streamed in the window.

For a minute I couldn't remember where I was.

Even with George the dog looking at me.

And then I did.

St. Simons Island.

The dangerous day.

I thought of the ship blowing up. Burning.

I thought of a submarine looking for more Americans.

"Let's go," George said. "We got work to do at the museum. Things to take back so we can get Mom and Dad home. I want to be a family again."

He licked his chops. His tongue went right over his nose.

"Wish I had a camera," I said and got out of bed. "I'd take a picture of that licking thing you do."

Linda didn't even move.

"Let her sleep," I said. "It was a terrible night."

George went to Linda's side of the bed. He sniffed her hair. Then licked her forehead.

"Your second kiss," I said.

George gave me a big grin.

We snuck out of the house.

On the front porch I said, "I wonder what kind of baby she's getting?"

"A boy," George said.

I closed the door. "Or maybe a girl," I said.

We went back to the beach.

The sun was hot.

If you looked at the trees and the sun and the houses, you'd never know something awful had happened.

But at the shore I could see the oil on the sand.

And there was still an awful smell.

Of burning.

I squinted to where I had first seen the SS *Oklahoma*.

Nothing but ocean.

A few men walked along the shore. They watched out to sea.

Were they searching for more men?

Looking for bodies?

Submarines?

"George! Gracie!"

Crowe? Where had he come from?

He ran toward us. He was mad. I could tell by the way he yelled.

George barked. He jumped up on me.

"Run, Gracie, run," he said. "To the dinghy. We have to get to it first."

He took off. I followed.

Crowe was fast for an old guy.

We had to be faster.

"Hurry, George," I said.

George got to the upside-down dinghy before me.

He dug around the boat. Throwing sand everywhere.

I could hear the waves slipping onto the shoreline. The sun sparkled on the sand.

I ran to George.

Crowe was so close.

George nudged the boat with his nose. "I can't tip it right-side up, Gracie," he said.

I tried to lift the dinghy. It was too heavy.

"Get on top, George," I said.

George looked at me.

His dark hair was white from where he had been digging. His muzzle, right up to his eyes, was covered in sand.

"I'm saving you a spot, Gracie," he said. He jumped up on the time machine dinghy. The boat trembled and rose in the air.

A foot off the ground. Two feet.

My heart thumped.

It was hard to breathe.

What a sight.

A huge dog.

On an upside down boat.

That floated in the air.

Crowe reached for me but missed.

"Hurry, Gracie," George said. Yelling.

I grabbed ahold of the dinghy. Tried to crawl on.

The time machine turned in slow motion. Dipped a little.

I clung to the side. Pulled myself up. George tugged at my dress. Helping me.

Crowe leaped into the air. He caught the dinghy with both hands. Pulled himself up.

"He's on," I said. The time machine spun faster.

And faster.

George barked. And nipped. And scratched at Crowe's hands.

"This. Is. My. Machine," Crowe said. He got one foot up.

George let out a bark so big I had to cover my ears.

I pushed Crowe's foot away.

George nipped at Crowe's fingers.

Crowe fell.

I wrapped my arms around George.

Tight.

The boat was so high now, I could see all the water. Shining like a mirror in my eyes.

Then ZOOM! we were in a black hole.

CHAPTER 11

Rowing Home

The time machine jerked to a stop.

Gracie fell into me. "Umppff," she said. "Why's it so dark all of a sudden?"

I heard Grandpa's voice. "George. Gracie," he said. "Are you in there?"

Then a Z-I-I-I-I-P sound.

Light flooded into . . . whatever we were in.

Grandpa peeked in. "Hi, kids," he said. "Feeling a little squished?"

The time machine had turned into a duffel bag. A big one. Me and Gracie were stuffed inside. Like dirty clothes.

A shoe smashed against my cheek. A slip-on.

"What the heck, Gracie?" I said. "Why'd you take your shoe off?"

"It's not my shoe," she said. She stood. "It's Crowe's. It came off when I pushed him off the dinghy."

We stepped out into Grandpa's fix-it shop.

"Hey—I'm me again," I said. I patted my arms. My legs. "Too bad."

I kind of liked being a dog. Having super powers.

Grandpa wrapped us both in a big hug. He held on like he hadn't seen us in forever. Even though we had only been gone a few seconds to him.

I was glad to see him too. "We're okay, Grandpa," I said.

"I was so afraid for you this trip," he said. "What was the dangerous day?"

"You won't believe it, Grandpa," Gracie said. She talked fast. "A submarine attacked Lonnie's ship. So me and George and Linda had to find him—"

"Gracie—" I said. But she didn't stop.

She inched closer to Grandpa. Licked her lips. Her eyes opened wide.

And she told every bit of the story. About our dangerous day. Every bit.

Grandpa backed into a chair. He sat down. Rubbed his face.

Gracie kept on talking.

I watched Grandpa. He looked like vanilla pudding. White and shaky.

"Gracie, Grandpa doesn't look so good," I said.

She still didn't stop. Her voice got higher and louder at the scariest parts.

When she took a breath, I said, "Gracie, STOP," and waved my hands in front of her. "You scared Grandpa."

"Oh," she said. "I'm sorry, Grandpa." She put her hand on his shoulder. "Me and George got home, though. We didn't get hurt or anything. We're happily ever after. Right?"

"It's okay, Gracie," Grandpa said. He had sweat on his forehead. "That *was* a dangerous day. I'm glad—and a little surprised—you're both safe."

Grandpa still looked like vanilla pudding. The kind that's been left out on the table all day.

"Kids," he said. He took a deep breath. "I've been thinking. I love your parents as much as you do. So we have to help them. But I love *you* too . . ."

He stopped.

Gracie pinched her locket between her fingers.

My glasses slipped down my nose.

"That's why I've decided to go with you on your next trip," Grandpa said.

"You can't," I said. "You'll get stuck in time."

"I can. And I will," Grandpa said. Now his face was like a cement wall. Not moving an inch. "Besides. If I get stuck, we'll all be together. We can figure it out. TO-GETH-ER."

Gracie chewed on her lip. Glanced at me. "George?" she said.

I shook my head because what could I do?

taptap tap-tap taptap tap-tap

Grandpa jumped. "Where's my pencil?"

We all scrambled to find it. I looked on the floor.

taptap tap-tap taptap tap-tap

Gracie ran to Grandpa's desk. Opened the top drawer.

taptap tap-tap taptap tap-tap

Grandpa felt around his ears. "Got it," he said.

He wrote the message on the back of an envelope.

"We're so . . . proud . . . of you . . . kids . . . Everyone's . . . home?"

"Yes . . ." Grandpa tapped an answer back. "We're all . . . here . . . together . . . Where are you?"

The machine was quiet.

Quiet.

Quiet.

"I wish they would talk some more," Gracie said.

"Me too," I said. I got lonely for Mom and Dad then. I thought about Maybelline and Lonnie and Linda. Linda!

"Hey, Gracie," I said. "We should call Linda. She'd be way old now. But I bet she's still alive. Let's find her number."

"Not this late," Grandpa said. "It's after midnight. But when your folks come home, we'll call her. Invite her over." He ruffled my hair.

"When Mom and Dad get home," Gracie said, "we'll stay up a whole week and talk and talk and talk." Her eyes got all shiny.

When Mom and Dad get home. I pushed my glasses up. And watched the map.

Because that light was going to blink. It would tell us where our parents were.

Any minute. It always did, right about now.

Gracie watched too.

So did Grandpa.

A red light flashed.

It blinked.

Blinked.

Blinked some more.

"Mom and Dad," said Gracie.

My stomach rolled around like a bowling ball. "It's time to go," I said.

"Remember, I'm going with you this time," said Grandpa. "No arguments."

He took my hand. And Gracie's. "Okay?"

"Okay, Grandpa," I said.

Gracie nodded.

We stepped up to the map.

THE END . . . OR IS IT?

A Dangerous Day in Georgia

"Hi. This is Gracie."

"And I'm George. We're going to tell you the true story of the sinking of the *SS Oklahoma* on April 8, 1942. Off the coast of St. Simons Island, Georgia. I'm going to start. Right Gracie?"

"Right, George."

"Um . . . it's a great story . . . you'll love it . . . so . . ."

"Go on, George. The kids are waiting."

"I don't know how to start, Gracie."

"Just open your mouth. Something will jump out. You know how you are, George."

"Yeah. I'll try that . . . It was a dark and stormy night in Georgia."

"No it wasn't, George."

"Well, it was dark anyway. Everybody on St. Simons was asleep. Little did they know the danger creeping toward them from the dark ocean."

"Oooh. I like the spooky beginning, George. Don't forget to tell them it was after midnight on April 8."

"So now you already told them, Gracie."

"Hee hee. I guess I did."

"Let me tell this part, okay Gracie?"

"I'm locking my lips, George. Lock, lock."

"Throw away the key, Gracie."

"Mmm mmm mm mmm. Mmm mm?"

"Yep, I can finish now. Thanks, Gracie. Like I said, it was a dark night but not stormy. The date was April 8, 1942. On a Wednesday. Four months earlier the United States had entered World War II because of the attack on Pearl Harbor. All the people on St. Simons Island and everywhere else in Georgia were asleep. Everybody, that is, except for Captain Reinhard Hardegen."

"Mm mm mmmm."

"Gracie says she's scared thinking about it. Close your eyes, why don't you? So Captain Hardegen's monster submarine swam around in the water. Looking for a Liberty Ship to sink with one of its torpedos."

"Mmmm mmm mmmm mm mmm, Mmmmmm."

"You're ruining my whole story, Gracie. She wants me to tell you that Liberty Ships belonged to the United States Merchant Marines. They carried oil and gasoline and ammunition and stuff like that to American soldiers during the war."

"Oh gosh, George. I said tell them that Captain Hardegen's submarine was called U-123. The 'U' stands for *unterseeboot*. That's German for 'undersea boat.' Or you can say *u-boot* for short."

"You didn't throw the key away, did you Gracie?"

"Nope. I stuck it in my pocket. For later."

"Anyway . . . The moon was bright that night and shining on the *SS Oklahoma*. So Captain Hardegen spotted it out in the water. Not too far from St. Simons. He moved in, aimed, and shot a torpedo. The ship sunk. Nineteen Merchant Marines died and most of them were asleep at the time."

"I hate war, George."

"Me too, Gracie. The worst part of the story is that Captain Hardegen took off and sunk another Liberty Ship a few miles away. In the ocean on the other end of St. Simons. The *Esso Baton Rouge*. Three men died on that ship. Then he came back and shot at the *SS Oklahoma* again."

"This is a sad story, George. It makes me cry."

"Here's a box of tissues, Gracie."

"Thanks, George. Can I tell the good part now?"

"Yeah, but hand me that tissue box first."

"Here you go, George. Okay, when the *SS Oklahoma* exploded, the sound was so loud it broke house windows. And rumbled the island. The people on St. Simons woke up and ran to the beach. There, in the ocean, they saw the burning ship.

The Georgia Coast Guard was already heading out to save the Merchant Marines in the water. The people on the beach jumped in their boats and followed after them.

Charles Candler was part of the Georgia Coastguard. He used his yacht to help with the rescue. Charles Candler's family owned the Coca-Cola company before the war, you know."

"So he could pass out Cokes to everybody on the beach, right Gracie?"

"Not funny, George."

"Sorry. But that is so cool that everybody ran out to help, Gracie. How did they know if the German submarine was gone? I mean, he could have torpedoed their boats too, right?"

"I don't know about that, George. But the people on St. Simons were brave for sure. Did I tell you they rescued a little yellow dog from one of the ships?"

"Aaahhh. Cute."

"I know, right George? After the attack on April 8, President Roosevelt made everybody on the east coast of the United States do blackouts at night. To protect them from submarines shooting torpedoes at the shore. And in case German planes flew over to bomb their towns."

"What's a blackout, Gracie? Like painting everything black?"

"You call yourself the brains of the family, George? Guess again."

"Okay. Blackout . . . like blacking something out . . . Oh. I get it. They had to turn out all their lights at night. Including their car lights."

"Sort of. They had to cover all their windows with thick curtains at night so the light wouldn't shine through. They couldn't use their car lights either or other outside lights after dark. The people in England gave them some good ideas about doing blackouts."

"Because England got bombed a lot in World War II. I know that story, Gracie."

"It's a good one. Too bad we don't have time to tell it. Say goodbye, George."

"Goodbye, George."

"Hi-lar-ious."

Georgia State Facts

- **Statehood:** January 2, 1788, the fourth state to ratify the Constitution of the United States
- **Origin of the Name "Georgia":** Georgia was named for King George II of England, a.k.a. George Augustus, King of Great Britain and Ireland, 1683–1760.
- **State Capital:** Atlanta
- **State Flag:** Georgia's state flag was adopted in 2003. It is based on the first national flag of the Confederacy, the "Stars and Bars." The state coat of arms is in the center of a circle of thirteen stars, which represent Georgia and the original, twelve other colonies that formed the United States. Beneath the coat of arms is the national motto: "In God We Trust."
- **State Nickname:** "Empire State of the South," "Peach State"
- **State Song:** "Georgia on My Mind"
- **State Motto:** "Wisdom, Justice, and Moderation"
- **State Flower:** Cherokee Rose
- **State Tree:** Live Oak
- **State Bird:** Brown Thrasher

- **State Insect:** Honeybee
- **State Color:** Georgia doesn't have a state color
- **State Fruit:** Peach

Georgia
State Curiosities

- The Okefenokee Swamp straddles the Georgia/Florida state line. It covers 400,000 acres and is the largest freshwater and black water wilderness swamp in North America. It is the home for hundreds of species of birds and wildlife, including several endangered species.

- Saint Marys, Georgia, is the second oldest city in the nation.

- The pirate Edward "Blackbeard" Teach made a home on Blackbeard Island, Georgia.

- The Chicken Capital of the World is in Gainesville, Georgia, where it is illegal to eat chicken with a fork.

- Georgia is the nation's number one producer of the three Ps—peanuts, pecans, and peaches.

- Every year Hawkinsville, Georgia, holds the famous "Shoot the Bull" barbecue championship. People from all over Georgia and surrounding states come to enter their tasty recipes in the cook-off. The money raised goes toward finding a cure for Down syndrome.

- Cordele, Georgia, claims to be the watermelon capital of the world.
- Coca-Cola was invented in May 1886 by Dr. John S. Pemberton in Atlanta, Georgia. Coca-Cola was also first sold at a soda fountain in Jacob's Pharmacy in Atlanta.
- Marshall Forest in Rome, Georgia, is the only natural forest in the United States that sits right inside the city limits.
- Jimmy Carter, the 39th president of the United States, lives in Plains, Georgia.
- The world's largest sculpture is carved into Stone Mountain near Atlanta, Georgia. The sculpture is a picture of Stonewall Jackson, Jefferson Davis, Robert E. Lee, and Robert E. Lee's horse, Traveler.
- The first college in the world that agreed to grant degrees to women is Wesleyan College in Macon, Georgia.

Meet the Authors

Cheri Pray Earl writes the voice of George in the *Just In Time* series. She says that raising four sons makes her an expert at writing boys. She has an M.A. in Creative Writing from Brigham Young University and has taught college writing and literature for over twenty years; in her other life, she writes novels for young adults and adults. She has four sons and four daughters-in-law, one daughter and one son-in-law, five grandchildren (with more on the way), two dogs, and a cat. Cheri lives with her husband, Jeff, in Utah.

Carol Lynch Williams is the author of more than 25 books for kids and teen readers. She runs Writing and Illustrating for Young Readers, has an MFA in Writing for Children and Adolescents from Vermont College, and writes on an active blog with fellow writers Ann Dee Ellis and Kyra Leigh Williams (www.throwingupwords.wordpress.com). She teaches creative writing at Brigham Young University. Her books include *The Chosen One*, *Glimpse*, *Miles from Ordinary*, and *Waiting*.

Signed, *Sky Harper*, and *The Haven* were published in 2014, as well as *Sister, Sister*, a Familius book. She is proudest of her five daughters who are Carol's most perfect creative effort, ever. She and Cheri have been best friends for more than 20 years.

Meet the Illustrator

Manelle Oliphant graduated from BYU-Idaho with her illustration degree. She loves illustrating historical stories and fairytales. She lives with her husband in Salt Lake City, Utah. You can see her work and download free coloring pages on her website at www.manelleoliphant.com.

Where will the time machine land next? Get a sneak peak at:

just-in-time-books.com

You'll also find tons of fun ways to learn more about state history and explore the *Just in Time* books.

Don't Miss George and Gracie's Other Adventures

BOOK ONE:

The Rescue Begins
in Delaware

BOOK TWO:

Sweet Secrets in
Pennsylvania

BOOK THREE:

The Wizard of
Menlo Park, New Jersey

JUST-IN-TIME-BOOKS.COM

CPSIA information can be obtained at www.ICGtesting.com
Printed in the USA
BVOW01s2306100914

366179BV00002B/2/P